# Red Wind and Thunder Moon

# Red Wind and Thunder Moon
# Max Brand

University of Nebraska Press, Lincoln and London

Earlier versions of this work were published under the titles 'Red Wind and Thunder Moon' by George Owen Baxter in *Western Story Magazine* (8/27/27) and 'Thunder Moon – Pale Face' by George Owen Baxter in *Western Story Magazine* (9/17/27). 'Red Wind and Thunder Moon.' Copyright © 1927 by Street & Smith Publications, Inc. Copyright © renewed 1955 by Dorothy Faust. 'Thunder Moon – Pale Face.' Copyright © 1927 by Street & Smith Publications, Inc. Copyright © renewed 1955 by Dorothy Faust. Acknowledgment is made to Condé Nast Publications, Inc., for their coopera-tion. Published by arrangement with Golden West Literary Agency. All rights reserved. Manufactured in the United States of America. ♾ The paper in this book meets the minimum requirements of American National Standard for Information Sciences – Permanence of Paper for Printed Library Materials, ANSI Z39.48-1984. Library of Congress Cataloging-in-Publication Data. Brand, Max, 1892–1944. Red Wind and Thunder Moon / Max Brand. p. cm. ISBN 0-8032-1268-2 (cl: alk. paper) 1. Indians of North America—Fiction. I. Title. PS3511.A87R43 1996 813'.52—dc20 95-43100 CIP The present text is based on the author's original typescript and this book appears now for the first time as the author wrote it. Max Brand™ has been registered as a trademark by the U.S. Patent Office and cannot be used without express written permission.

# Contents

# Part One

# Two Crafty Traders

When Walking Horse came to visit the Suhtai band of the Cheyennes over which Big Hard Face was the leading chief, it was an event of great importance. Not that such visits were at all rare of a warrior passing for a time, or even permanently, into another of the ten allied bands of the Cheyenne nation, but Walking Horse was no common brave. Among the Omissis of the Cheyennes he was the very foremost and leading name. He had built up such fame supported on such hardy achievements in battle that it was almost as though half the power of the Omissis, condensed into the person of this one man, had come to sit down among the Suhtais.

His visit was also made significant by various details of his conduct. In the first place, though he was absolutely the principal chief among his tribesmen, he came alone with no following whatever. In the second place, he came among the Suhtai and found there a number of old friends, former associates in battle, grave and celebrated figures. He visited in one teepee and then in another. He talked of the hunt, of the war trails on which he had ridden with them and with others, of the prosperity of the Cheyennes, and of the devilishness of the Pawnees. Yet never a word did he say of the cause of his visit.

All of this was very singular, of course. The outer world, which has mistaken the shyness of the Indian among strangers for taciturnity, perhaps will feel inclined to say that this essential silence was the nature of the man and of all his peers but, as a matter of fact, the Indian talks as fast as running water when he is among tried companions. Even so Walking Horse of the Omissis said not a word of the reason for this visit. He was among them for a fortnight, and still not a word of explanation was given! Whispers of wonder ran back and forth through the camp.

Then came a band of three well-known warriors from the Omissis. They saw their chief. When they proposed to him a promising plan for a raid upon the Sioux, Walking Horse turned to them a deaf ear. After that, they asked him how long he would be absent from his people. They received no rejoinder. Further than this, mystified, hurt, and desperate, they drifted here and there among the Suhtai lodges and asked cautiously: what was the purpose that kept their chief so long from home? Affairs of the greatest importance were up for discussion in the councils of the Omissis. Why did not their war chief come home?

Of course, the Suhtai had no answer. The suspense grew greater and greater. What was the purpose in the mind of this great man? Had his feelings been wounded by some slight received by his followers? Did he contemplate joining himself to the Suhtai permanently? It made the Suhtai chiefs scowl – not one of them wished to be elbowed from his place by such an addition to the roll of great ones in the camp – as it made the common warriors glad, for many and many a youth yearned to follow such a famous leader.

So a month passed. Then Walking Horse went out from the village to the place where Big Hard Face was watching his great herd of ponies grazing. Wrapped in their robes, the two chiefs stood side by side and regarded the horses.

'You are rich, *Mahk-he-kon-in-i*,' said the visitor.

'I am rich,' admitted Big Hard Face, with a grunt of satisfaction.

'The horses are not as big in stature as they are in numbers,' went on the Omissis.

'They are greater in heart than in body,' replied Big Hard Face. 'Look at them again.'

The other made a little pause and pretended to look. Long before this he had examined the herd in the greatest detail and saw that there was not a single weed in the lot. Small they might be on the whole, but there was not one to whose hardihood and speed a chief of chiefs might not be proud to trust himself and all his fortunes. Surely a rich strain of blood was represented here.

'I have looked,' said Walking Horse at last. 'They are very good,' he admitted.

'They are Comanche horses,' said Big Hard Face, concealing his satisfaction as well as he could. 'There is not one among them that is not a Comanche.'

Of all the tribes that rode upon the plains the Comanches were famous for the excellence of their mounts. Perhaps it was because on their many raids into old Mexico they had seized the cream of the Spanish horses again and again and so purified the strain of their herds. Perhaps it was that the desert life on their southern ranges tempered and hardened their horseflesh. At any rate, mounted upon their ponies their stroke was like the stroke of lightning and, if they failed, the hostile tribes could not pursue them in their flight.

'All Comanches. All Comanches,' murmured Walking Horse. 'Then you have given a great treasure for so many.'

'I have not given,' said Big Hard Face, touching the beadwork which encrusted his robe so richly. 'I have not given so much as the value of a single one of these beads.'

'They were all taken in war, then?' asked the other, drawing in his breath a little.

'They were taken in war, brother.'

Walking Horse regarded the older man for a moment. Big Hard Face was well advanced in age. His strength had turned heavy upon him. But he had not yet withered and grown weak, yet no one could imagine him swooping down on the agile Comanches in distant raids.

'They are gifts,' said the old man in explanation. 'All the gifts of Thunder Moon, my son.'

'One does not need to be a hawk to see Thunder Moon on the earth,' said the Omissis. 'One does not need the ears of an owl to hear his name. Because of him, how many lodges are empty in the camps of the Comanches and how many of their young wives gash their flesh and cut their hair short and sit in the dust to mourn? If I had a wish to buy from you fifty of these horses of the Comanches, what price would you place upon them, brother?'

Big Hard Face gathered his robe a little closer about him and cast a glance brighter than fire at his companion. The lust of the trader was hot in his soul.

'That is a thing to consider,' he said.

'A horse is a horse,' replied the Omissis, 'and a woman is no more than a woman. These things all have their price.'

'Would you ask an eagle for the value of his wings?' asked Big Hard Face, a most cunning bargainer. 'If I wish to send out the best of my young men on a great raid, when they must fly far and fast, I lead out these horses of mine. I place the young warriors on their backs. It is then as though I had placed them on the back of the wind. They ride out. They are so fast that their enemies cannot see them in mid-day. They strike. They count a hundred coups. Then they return to my village and before their faces a great cloud of dust rolls up to the heart of the sky. It is raised by the hoofs of the horses which they drive back to me.' He waved his hand again toward his herd of horses. 'Now you ask me,' he said, 'at what price I will be willing to sell fifty of these?'

'Horses are good,' replied the Omissis, taking the time-honored track of all traders making a good bargain, 'but so are rich robes covered with beads and robes painted by cunning hands. New strong guns are good. So are much powder and lead and keen knives and sugar and coffee!'

Big Hard Face grinned and showed two or three large fangs in the black shapeless slit of his mouth. 'They are good,' he said. 'Sugar is good!' He licked his lips and drew in a great breath.

'Pounds and pounds of sugar,' said the Omissis cleverly, 'and knives, guns, robes. It is only necessary to name the amount. You are rich, Big Hard Face. Neither am I a poor man.'

'When a man stands on a cliff,' said Big Hard Face, 'one step is life and one is death. There is no need for hurry. Let us go back to my lodge and speak with Thunder Moon.'

Back toward the village they strolled. The wild heat of the midday was over. The shadows were reaching toward the east. From the river the shouts of the playing and swimming boys and young men rose into the air, echoing hollow from the face of the water. Girls were coming in with bundles of firewood broken or cut in the brush. Women were carrying up water. Smoke was going up from the lodges.

At the entrance to the village, they passed a burly Indian clad in a robe of great value, wearing a strange headdress which was the scalp of a wolf mounted with all the terribly grinning teeth. Beneath that uncouth gear there showed a thoughtful, meditative face. He was passing with his eyes upon the ground but, seeing Big Hard Face, he started and raised his hand.

'How!'

'How!' said Big Hard Face, and went on.

'I still wait,' said the man of the wolf's head.

Big Hard Face answered nothing but went rather more hurriedly on his way.

'Tell me, brother,' said the Omissis, who had listened with much curiosity to this brief exchange, 'was not that Spotted Bull, the chief among the medicine men of the Suhtai?'

'May he die without a scalp!' exclaimed Big Hard Face. 'May he die as naked as when he was born and the Pawnee wolves count coup on him three times. Why should he fix his teeth in a child of my teepee?'

'Ha,' murmured Walking Horse. 'Then he is not a friend to Thunder Moon?'

Big Hard Face sighed but, as though the matter were too great for words, he said no more of it, and the Omissis did not press the point. They came to the lodge of Big Hard Face and passed inside. Big Hard Face, as he passed in through the flap, uttered a little exclamation of disgust and displeasure. For squatted in the middle of the teepee with a flashing scraper in his hand, the son of the chief was hard at work preparing a small buffalo hide.

'Woman's work!' snorted Big Hard Face. 'Thunder Moon, do you forget that you are a man?'

# 2

# The Bargain Is Made

Thunder Moon shrugged his broad shoulders and did not turn his head. 'White Crow is old and tired,' he said. 'Besides, who would sit by the fire all day and make his lungs ache with smoke or tell stories until the tongue tires?' Saying this, he continued to work with the flashing tool, which was a shoulder-blade shaped for the grip of the hands. There was no vestige of clothing on him except for moccasins on his feet, a breech clout, and a narrow band which held back from his face the long shower of black hair that fell glistening over his shoulders and down his back almost to his hips. As he worked with the scraping bone, one could see why no man among all the tall Cheyennes dared to exchange cuffs with him, or wrestle with him hand to hand on equal terms. For though his arms were massive, they were alive with long, twisting tangles of muscle that swept without a break from shoulder to wrist, and the power across his shoulders knotted and leaped like so many hands being clenched hard beneath the skin.

Walking Horse took curious note of this figure. Though he had been many days among the Suhtai, still he had not had great opportunity for observing Thunder Moon. Thunder Moon did not go to the feasts. When the circle formed and the coup stick was passed, Thunder Moon would rise and stride from a teepee. He did not go where the old men talked in the evening.

'Thunder Moon!' exclaimed the old chief in a tone of command.

The young man turned and stood up. Seeing a guest, he greeted him gravely, flushing a little, and threw a robe about his great shoulders.

Big Hard Face was terribly displeased but he swallowed his anger a little. He merely said: 'How can a man's work be done by a woman? Or a woman's work by a man?'

'Father,' replied Thunder Moon, 'tell me this: when a man strikes in a battle should his hand be heavy or light?'

'That is a child's question,' answered the chief.

'Very well,' said Thunder Moon, 'does the hand grow strong holding a pipe or dipping into the meat pot?'

'It is always like this,' said Big Hard Face gloomily, turning to the Omissis. 'There is no corner so narrow that he cannot talk his way out of it. There are more words and ways to his tongue than there are buffalo and their trails on the open plains. Now hear me, Thunder Moon. Walking Horse wishes to know the price of fifty of your horses. He is a guest. He is a famous man. Therefore we wish to make him a small price. Consider it, Thunder Moon.'

He made a little private sign to his son which, in a white man, might well have been replaced by a wink.

Thunder Moon considered. His two elders were seated. He remained standing, and with the butt of a battle spear he prodded at the earth. 'We do not wish to lose so many horses,' he said. 'Our guest is a famous man. Take fifty from our herd. You need them for the war path, I suppose? Take them, send out your young men on their backs. If some horses die on the trail, it is no matter. When the young men return, keep ten of the best for yourself and send back the remainder to me. I have spoken.'

It seemed as though Big Hard Face would choke during the latter part of this short speech. His color changed and his eyes started from his scarred, horribly deformed face. Still he dared not say no. It was beneath the dignity of any brave to deny a gift once proffered, but he writhed to and fro on his couch and hurriedly caught up a pipe that smoke might allay his injured feelings.

As for Walking Horse, no doubt he was familiar with the impulsive generosity of his race, but this was a kingly magnificence that was quite beyond his comprehension. His eyes burned for a moment and, to mask that greedy fire, he glanced down to the ground. He cleared his throat once or twice and then he began to make a speech. He declared, in many magnificent words, that he would be ashamed to ask a price and then get horses for nothing. One horse he would accept, partly because the Comanche strain was so glorious, but partly because every horse that Thunder Moon had taken from the enemy was a reminder to every Cheyenne of the glory of the taker. That glory grew every day. According to Walking Horse, as he warmed to his work, the whole nation of the Pawnees shuddered in their lodges when they so much as thought of Thunder Moon. The Comanches hushed the cries of their children with his dreadful name. Accordingly, Walking Horse would accept one pony, the meanest of the herd, as a souvenir of the great man. In the meantime he persisted, and begged Thunder Moon to name the price of fifty horses.

Under this shower of praise, Thunder Moon at first stood straight, then winced. He turned a bright red – which the paleness of his face made more pronounced – and finally seemed to look for an avenue of escape. At last he said, with a bluntness of which no other Cheyenne assuredly would have been guilty:

'Your many words make me unhappy. Take whatever horse you please. But great praise means great blame.'

He turned to his father and bade Big Hard Face settle the terms if a price were to be made.

Big Hard Face could wait no longer. 'You see,' he said, 'that we do not wish to sell. The heart of Thunder Moon is like a rain cloud. It would dissolve in giving. But, since you will not take the gifts he offers,' the chief went on hurriedly, 'then I shall tell you a cheap price for such horses as run in our herd. One hundred good rifles and ten of the small guns that have six voices.' He indicated a revolver which hung from the post at the foot of Thunder Moon's couch. 'Also, much lead and powder, and ten good knives with edges that will not turn. Furthermore, we need some good painted robes and a suit covered with beads. The Omissis women make many of them. If you will do these things, then you may be sure that you shall have the fifty horses.'

Walking Horse considered these demands with blinking eyes and a shudder. 'Brother,' he said sadly, 'you ask for enough guns to arm a whole tribe.'

'The Omissis are rich,' said Big Hard Face coldly, 'and all men know that Walking Horse is the richest of his tribe. His horses make the earth tremble as they gallop together. Two tall and broad teepees cannot hold the mass of his saddles and guns and beaded clothes and knives and other treasures.'

'Ah, brother,' murmured the visitor, 'rumor is full of lies. I am not so rich.'

He looked appealingly at them in turn. Big Hard Face endured that appeal with an unmoved countenance, but Thunder Moon frowned at the ground and bit his lip. It was plain that his father's bargaining had shamed him.

'However,' said the Omissis suddenly, 'if I am not so rich, neither am I poor. You shall have everything as you ask. In return, I shall want something more than just the fifty horses.'

'Speak,' said Big Hard Face, his eyes narrowing to shrewdness again. There was still a faraway light in them, as though already his glance were caressing the heap of weapons for which he had bargained.

'It is a small thing,' said the other. 'In my teepee there is a thing which I wish to give to Thunder Moon, to be taken into his lodge and cherished. Let Thunder Moon give me his promise that he will accept it. Then I shall go to make the long journey to the fort of the white man and bring back all that your hearts desire.'

'You are kind,' said Big Hard Face instantly, 'and my son accepts your kindness.'

'No,' put in Thunder Moon, 'I have no need of gifts which I do not know. I have a horse to ride, a gun to shoot, and a spear to stab with. What more does a Cheyenne ask of the Sky People?'

'Boy,' said his father, 'you speak like a fool. You shame me before Walking Horse. Tell him at once that whatever he brings, you will take and keep it well to honor him!'

Thunder Moon looked narrowly at the Omissis, leaning forward a little and seeming to probe the very soul of the stranger.

'It is well,' he said finally. 'My father commands me. I give my word to Walking Horse.'

There had been a great tension in the expression of the Omissis up to this time. Now it was as though a burden had been cast from his mind. He stood up and, making some remark about the distance of the journey which he had to perform, he left the teepee almost at once. Five minutes later he had departed from the camp of the Suhtai.

He left a gloomy scene behind him, where Thunder Moon stared at his foster father.

'There was more wealth put in our hands,' said Big Hard Face, 'than any Suhtai ever has seen in one heap before and been able to call his own. You would have thrown it away! Thunder Moon, you are a child and you grow no older with the years.'

'Tell me,' said Thunder Moon, 'has not Walking Horse acted like a fool to accept your price without bargaining?'

Big Hard Face smiled with the greatest satisfaction. 'Wisdom is richer than wealth and cunning thoughts are turned into strong horses,' he said.

'Yet,' said Thunder Moon, 'Walking Horse is not a fool, but a wise chief and a ruler over chiefs, and a rich man as well.'

Big Hard Face was quite silent, frowning.

'You may be sure,' said the younger man, 'that whatever he gives to us will be a thing worse than poison to him.'

'Still you have many words,' said Big Hard Face. 'But words are not medicine. If there is poison in his teepee, would he not throw it away?'

'You will see,' said Thunder Moon in reply. 'Unless Walking Horse is a fool, I know that he came to us not to buy horses, but to make us take this precious gift. When we receive it, may the Sky People give us strength and wisdom.'

# 3

# All Medicine Is Foolish

Three important events kept the mission of Walking Horse and his expected return well in the background during the following weeks. In the first place, the tribe moved camp. In the second place, Spotted Bull fell out with Big Hard Face and Thunder Moon. In the third place, Falling Stone, a young Pawnee brave, made the first of his famous excursions into Cheyenne territory and crossed swords with Thunder Moon.

As for the camp removal, it was no more important than such events usually were. It called for the making of medicine and the making of the medicine brought Spotted Bull to the lodge of Big Hard Face. There they sat talking amicably, until the medicine man turned the conversation into other channels.

'I have waited for three months,' said the medicine man, 'and still Thunder Moon keeps far from me. I never see him in my teepee. On the walls of my lodge hang suits of rich beadwork and I have painted robes and knives and guns given to me by the braves of the Suhtai, but I have nothing from the hand of Thunder Moon.'

Big Hard Face made a slight grimace. 'My son shall remember you,' he said. 'Go home, and you will find three horses at your teepee. They will let you know that Thunder Moon is your friend.'

'A gift that is asked for is meat that chokes the gullet,' said the medicine man grimly. 'It is not for added riches that I sorrow. It is because the young men come to me and say, 'From whom did these good things come?' Then I name the givers. Behold, all the brave men of our tribe are then named and many famous men from among all of the Cheyennes whose children and wives I have healed, from whose fortunes I have taken curses, and whose guns I have given power on the war path. At last I must stop. They look at me in wonder. They say: "What is the gift of our greatest warrior, our hero with the heart of a charging bull, our wisest councilor who has the strongest hand and who keeps the richest teepee? What is the gift of Thunder Moon?" Then I am silent. I hang my head, and the men go away, wondering.'

Spotted Bull had retained his calm, but only through a considerable effort. Now he was breathing hard. He could hardly compel himself to take the pipe which Big Hard Face had had trouble filling and had passed to him.

'Consider the soul of a young man,' said Big Hard Face. 'It is like the wind that roves through the sky. It blows here and it blows there, not because one quarter of the heaven is better than another, but because it has an idle way.'

The medicine man snorted as he blew out smoke to the earth and smoke to the sky. 'Tell me this,' he answered. 'The foolish youths of our tribe are like colts, throwing up their heels and running from grass to water and from water to grass, but Thunder Moon has a mind that thinks. When he looks into the face of a man, he is like one who reads the sign of a trail. All that he does, he does with a good reason, even though his reasons are not anything like the reasons of the rest of the Suhtai.'

The anger of Spotted Bull was growing. His host feebly fumbled here and there with his wits, but he could think of nothing that might appease his guest.

Spotted Bull continued: 'Is my medicine bad? What else has given good fortune to Big Hard Face? What has turned the weapons of his enemies away from his breast when he rode to war? Now there is a greater medicine in his teepee, men say!' With a malignant smile, he pointed to a glittering thing made of yellow metal. It hung from the central pole of the teepee, shaped roughly and rudely into the semblance of a human arm.

Big Hard Face looked in the same direction. There was much respect in his voice as he said: 'That is a piece of The Yellow Man, the greatest medicine that the Comanches owned. Has not their luck left them since Thunder Moon carried their medicine away from them? Have they not run from before the faces of the Suhtai? Has not Thunder Moon prospered in all things because of that medicine, brother?'

A deep, guttural exclamation from Spotted Bull showed Big Hard Face that he had touched a most tender point. 'I know it!' said the medicine man. 'That was the knowledge that the spirits whispered to me when they said that an enemy was lodged in the teepee of Big Hard Face. The Yellow Man has always done mischief to the Cheyennes. When he was with the Comanches, he turned their bullets into the hearts of our warriors. Now he only can turn Suhtai against Suhtai. Always he has been the enemy of my tribe! Throw away that cursed token, brother. Give it to me. Let me purify it. Let me hang it in my tent. I shall accept the danger that comes out of it.'

He rose from his place, touched the symbol, weighed it in his hand. 'Yes,' he said. 'I shall take it from you.'

'Brother,' said the chief in a dry voice, 'take heed for yourself. Do not touch it. My son would be angry.'

'The anger of a man,' replied Spotted Bull, 'is nothing to me. Neither yours nor your son's. I have to do with such great spirits, Big Hard Face, that if I call them now, they would leap down out of the sky and turn you and all that is in your teepee into mist. The people who passed would see no more than a big smoke going upwards from this pipe of mine.'

He said this solemnly and Big Hard Face, listening with starting eyes, shuddered and sighed.

'But, I am your friend,' went on the medicine man who saw that he had made a point, 'and I wish to be the friend of Thunder Moon. I have been his friend all these days, without gift or without kindness from him. I have prayed for his success on the war path. I have offered up sacrifice. I have taken out the sacred medicine pipes for his sake. I have no reward. I have not gone among the people and said to them in times of misfortune, "You are hungry and cold, but may that not be because you keep in your midst a man who makes strange medicine? A man who speaks with the tongue of a Suhtai, but whose heart is not the heart of a Suhtai." '

He paused. Big Hard Face sat up stiffly. 'What lying spirit has told you that his spirit is not the spirit of a Suhtai? Is he not my son?'

The medicine man could not restrain a grin of triumph and malice. 'Is your skin the color of my skin?' he said.

'That is true.'

'We are Suhtai, brother. But the skin of Thunder Moon is the pale skin of a white man. He is not your son. He is a stranger. His heart is a stranger's heart.'

The eyes of Big Hard Face flickered from side to side. If ever danger were written visibly on the face of a man, it was written on the face of Big Hard Face. 'This is not good talking,' he said huskily. 'Brother, beware!'

'I remember when you left the camp,' said Spotted Bull. 'It was many years ago and you were gone many, many days. When you came back, you had the child with you. You took him into your teepee. You got him a Suhtai name. He was a member of the tribe. But he is a white man. He is not one of us. How would it be, Big Hard Face, if I told these things to Thunder Moon himself?'

'If you separate a father from a son,' replied Big Hard Face ominously, 'because of the wrong words which your spirits have told you. . . .' He could not say anything more. His eyes, however, were fire.

The medicine man continued smoothly: 'I have no wish to make trouble. That is for the medicine of The Yellow Man yonder to do. I work against him. I try to keep peace in our city. I make our young warriors like brothers on the trail. Only . . . I tell you again, let Thunder Moon come to me. Let him open his heart to me like a child to a father. All still may be well between us. All still may be well.' Having said this, he got up at once and left the teepee, gathering his dignity about him like a robe. Big Hard Face remained, lost in gloomy reflections.

Thunder Moon came in from the hunt with three horses loaded with antelope meat, for when did he return empty-handed? The old chief then sent White Crow away from the lodge and sat down beside his son and talked with him before the blood of the hunt was washed from his hands. Not all of the conversation with Spotted Bull was repeated, but enough was said to explain that the teepee and all in it, especially Thunder Moon, were in danger of the terrible wrath of the medicine man. Their bodies might be twisted with deformities. Their horses might be stolen. Their arms might grow powerless. The bullets of the enemy might be turned into their hearts, their scalps hung at the belt of Pawnee warriors, and their souls left to wander miserably up and down the winds of the earth until at last they dwindled, grew thin, and disappeared forever.

When the young man had heard it, he answered gravely.

'Father, you are old and you are wise. You know how to speak before the council. You understand how to hunt the buffalo. You know many things, and every day I sit at your knee like a child and drink in your words and your wisdom. As for Spotted Bull, and all the doctors of our tribe and of all other tribes and the medicine that they make, I think they are no more than scoundrels or fools, and that their medicine is folly. I will not have it.'

Big Hard Face hastily threw a sweet grass on the fire and went through the motions of bathing himself in the purifying smoke. He did the same for his son. 'Do not speak like this,' he complained. 'Words may be more dangerous than Pawnee bullets. It is not much to go to the teepee of Spotted Bull and say that you are his friend. It will cost you nothing.'

'It will cost me a lie,' said Thunder Moon.

'It will cost you only a word.'

'Look!' said the youth. 'Now, I am as free as any man could wish to be. I go where I will over the prairie. I pass in and I pass out from the village, and I am my own master, except when you command me. You are the chief of our tribe. I do not even belong to any of the soldier bands. No man can compel me to do one thing if I choose to do another. Now you want me to make a slave of my mind to Spotted Bull. I shall not be his slave. I laugh at him and, if he crosses me, I shall laugh in his face and beat him into his teepee. He is a villain and a fool. You want to make me worse than a squaw, worse than the stupid white men who are not able to live under the sky and who have to have roofs over their heads, making their heaven out of wood. No, Father, I must be free. All medicine is foolishness.'

'Do you never pray?' asked the old man, angry but baffled.

'Yes,' said Thunder Moon. 'I pray to the Sky People. They send a shining cloud across the face of the heavens. I know that they have heard my prayer. It always has been so since I was a boy. I shall go out and ask them now if I have been wrong.'

# 4

# Troubled Spirits

Beyond the village, seated on his horse on the top of a hill, Thunder Moon looked up to the sky and raised his hands. So much was seen by Big Hard Face. For an entire half hour the young man remained in that position, though the sun must almost have blinded his eyes. Then forming suddenly in the middle of the sky, a cloud of a dazzling whiteness appeared and blew softly down toward the northern horizon.

Big Hard Face watched no longer from the distance but went hastily back to his teepee, his mind revolving many doubts. Of the success of his foster child in war the whole tribe could bear witness. Of the wisdom of Thunder Moon all the council of the old men and the heroes could speak also. For what plan of war was considered unless Thunder Moon were in the camp to give his advice? So it had been from the days of his youth, and most particularly since that famous expedition against the Comanches which had brought back the arm of The Yellow Man from the southern riders.

Yet there were gaps in the strength of Thunder Moon. No man was so acutely aware of them as Big Hard Face. There had been a time when his life had been turned to a hell of misery. In those days the croaking voice of White Crow, his aunt and the only woman of his teepee, continually pointed out the weakness of the foster child. As she had said in those days, Thunder Moon never was one to endure pain like a brave Indian. Even as a young man, sudden agony could wring a cry from his lips. When the other young braves drew their belts tighter and endured famine on the trail, Thunder Moon grew faint, just as he grew faint if the race were long on foot. He did not have even the craft of a ten-year-old boy in reading the signs of the war trail. His eyes and his ears seemed to be half blinded or deafened. In all these matters he was lacking, and great matters they were.

He had worse faults and follies. He took no joy in slaying an enemy from ambush but, like a madman, he loved the battle only when he endured a peril in order to inflict an injury. In the middle of a battle had he not been known to go insane, like a witless creature, with battle passion and charge straight through the line of the enemy, shooting to the right and to the left? These indeed were things to be wondered at, but greater stupidity remained. To any sensible plains Indian, there were three necessary parts to battle. One was the counting of the coup. One was the slaying of the foe. And one was the taking of his scalp. Their importance was first the counting of the coup and second the taking of the scalp. Last of all was the actual slaying of the foeman. Yet with Thunder Moon these matters were reversed. He would not take a scalp. He would not have his clothes trimmed with scalp locks or hang them from the bridle of his horse. He declared that they were disgusting emblems. As for the counting of coup, he scorned the ceremony and announced that it had no meaning to touch the body of an enemy. But to kill – ah, that was a different matter!

Never had there been a Cheyenne in the remembrance of old Big Hard Face to match this adroit hunter of the Pawnees and the Comanches. Never had there been another to equal his list of the slain. In battle, the charge of Thunder Moon was like the charge of an entire squadron. The foe could not stand against him.

So he had virtues to balance against his faults. No Indian could handle a rifle with such remorseless skill. Few even possessed the new small revolvers which were so deadly in the possession of Thunder Moon. If mere boys could outlast him in a long run, not the most brilliant athlete could escape from him in a short sprint – just as the mountain lion overtakes the wolf, although it cannot run all day across the plains. So, too, he had such wisdom in council as made the old men wonder. He seemed able to read the minds of friends and foes. The same iron which seemed to nerve his hand for an encounter and make it resistless was no less in his wits.

Thunder Moon was so different from the rest of the tribesmen that he never could become a chief. Yet, he was so necessary to them that they could not imagine the Suhtai without his help. Because of him Big Hard Face had remained in his lofty position as leader of the tribe. Now, as the old chief revolved the words of the medicine man again and again, he wondered if it were not true that not only the skin but the soul of his foster child was white. If that were the case, might he not someday even return to his people?

Big Hard Face drew his robe about his face. There he sat, shrouded in darkness, when his son returned and announced in a quiet, cheerful voice that all was well. The Sky People approved of what he had said and done concerning Spotted Bull. They had sent him a visible sign not many moments before.

His father returned no answer for his soul was sore. During the days that followed, Big Hard Face waited for the danger to strike at him from the hand of the medicine man. He lacked the cunning to argue with his foster son. All he could do was endure and to hope for the best. The croaking voice of White Crow did not help him. Time had withered her, but it had not taken the strength from her sinewy arm or the deathless malice from her tongue. She had heard enough of the trouble between Thunder Moon and the medicine man. Her dry, dusty voice rattled out prophecies of evil for a long time to come.

Before any blow could be struck by Spotted Bull, who seemed to be waiting with an admirable patience for some approach from Thunder Moon, a blow of another sort struck the entire village. It was the first raid on them by Falling Stone. Still in the flower of his youth, Falling Stone had been known only a short time for being a rising young brave among the Pawnees. Obviously he had now reached such consideration among his tribesmen that they had sent him out with a considerable body of warriors. He stole up close to the Suhtai camp and, just with the setting of the sun, he rushed his horsemen up from the hollow by the river. Half the entire horse herd was swept away by that charge. Falling Stone led his warriors on to the outskirts of the village. There they rode down, slew, and counted coup upon more than twenty people, mostly women and children. But a death is a death, and a coup is a coup. All are equally honorable. All equally swell the fame of an Indian.

Behind the stampeded horses, Falling Stone and his warriors rushed away across the prairie. They had dealt the Cheyennes such a blow as they had not received in years from their traditional enemies. A vengeance party was assembled at once, all the best and the bravest of the young men. As a matter of course Thunder Moon was there to lead them.

There was only a hasty consultation with Spotted Bull. It was in this brief moment that he struck his blow. He came out in his full medicine regalia, a nightmare figure, and he chanted to the excited listeners a pretended revelation from the spirits. They bid the Suhtai no longer to follow the leadership of Thunder Moon – certainly not until he had been purified in the eyes of the Sky People for his sins.

At such a time as this, while a war party was actually arming in haste, there was no question of doubting the advice of the inspired prophet. With Standing Bear, the tried and trusted hero, to lead them, the war party rushed away on the trail of the Pawnees. Thunder Moon remained behind. He sat his horse before Spotted Bull. Women, children, and old men surrounded them.

'Spotted Bull,' he said, 'has my good fortune left me?'

'Alas, my son,' said the medicine man, 'what your sins have been, you know as well as I. The spirits tell me. Your heart tells you what you have done that is wrong.'

'Tell me, Spotted Bull. Am I to bring back none of the stolen horses, and are no Pawnees to fall under my rifle?' asked the youth.

'I have said it,' answered Spotted Bull, gathering his robe about him. 'It is only a fool who asks a man to repeat a thing that he has said once.'

Behind the medicine man, his uncle and his young nephew had guns in hand, ready to defend him in case Thunder Moon's proverbially heavy hand threatened to descend on Spotted Bull. Thunder Moon merely laughed, sitting at ease on the back of one of his Comanche ponies with a led horse beside him.

'I go on that trail,' he said. 'When I come back, I shall let the people see that Spotted Bull is a liar and a fool!'

He rode away into the night, leaving consternation behind him. Big Hard Face was lost in bewilderment and woe. What could be the outcome of this duel between his foster child and the most powerful medicine man in the tribe? He could not guess, but he gravely doubted. Every Suhtai prejudice would be on the side of Spotted Bull.

In fact, no sooner had the warrior departed than Spotted Bull began to rouse sentiment against Thunder Moon. Openly and in private he talked. The old men listened. The children gabbled the news about the village. The women could talk of nothing else. All that could be said against Thunder Moon was brought forth now – how as a boy he had failed in the test of courage by which the Cheyennes pass from boyhood to manhood and become worthy of the war trail so that, indeed, he could hardly be called a warrior at all. How pain frightened him. How he failed in his reverence to the spirits and offered them no sacrifice. How even in battle he would count no coups. He would take no scalps!

'Because he dares not!' said the medicine man. 'He has no medicine except the medicine that he stole from the Comanches, and that is poison for a true Cheyenne. This man has a white skin. He has a white heart. Let him go back to his own people.'

These words were reported in due course to Big Hard Face. If he had not heard them from rumor, he would have heard them from White Crow as she worked in the teepee.

'Woman,' thundered the chief in a fury at last, 'do you hate Thunder Moon?'

She raised her head and looked at him with bright, beady eyes. 'I am a Cheyenne!' she said.

'Is that an answer?' cried Big Hard Face. 'Am I not a Cheyenne, also?'

'I am a Cheyenne and a Suhtai,' she said.

Big Hard Face glared at her evilly for another moment and then he turned and rushed from the lodge into the darkness that waited for him outside – the darkness of the night and the darkness of his troubled spirit.

# 5

# Reaching Spears

For a whole day the eager horsemen of the Suhtai rushed across the plains on the hot trail of Falling Stone and the Pawnee warriors. Toward dusk of the second day they came to a shallow stream and began to ford it in haste. Nearly half of them were across when the ground before them quivered and the air was stirred by the rapid drumming of many hoofs.

Over the brow of the farther slope Falling Stone with all his warriors banded behind him drove down upon the Cheyennes. The Suhtai, disordered, tired from the long march, straggling here and there or heaped close together just as they had come out of the ford, did not think of resistance for a moment. They turned to flee and, as they fled, the bullets and the showered arrows of the Pawnees dealt death among them. The reaching spears stabbed them in the back. Right on into the water, which foamed with blood and with tramplings, the Pawnees charged. At a shrill command from their leader, they swerved suddenly away, back to the bank. From the cover of the shrubbery that lined the shore, all lying prostrate and taking secure aim, they pelted the yelling Cheyennes with bullets and with arrows again.

Undoubtedly there were enough Suhtai present to have lurched back across the stream and overwhelmed these daring horse thieves, but it was not Indian nature to make such a frontal attack. They might also have swung to either side and tried a flank of the Pawnees, but they had received a dreadful check. Fifty of their best and bravest lay dead, scalped, unburied behind them. Their bodies had been plundered, their sacred medicine bags gone, and their corpses flung into the river where they were rolled and tumbled and battered and hurried far away.

Plainly the medicine which accompanied the Suhtai upon this expedition was of little strength. Therefore the band turned sadly back toward the distant village. Even then, Falling Stone would not have done, but with a dozen of his best rifles he hung on the rear of the defeated host and quickly bagged a round half dozen laggards.

When had there been such another day as this for the Pawnees? When such another for the Suhtai band? On the farther shore of the river, secure beyond its waters, Falling Stone pitched his camp at last and prepared to give his men a full day of rest and rejoicing and feasting before they continued the march. All his braves had counted at least one brave, and great deeds unboasted are like poison in the soul of an Indian. Talk he must, and sing of his glory.

From the woods that crowned the slope, Falling Stone had trees cut and dragged down whole to the edge of the water. There the great fire was lighted. Around it smaller camp fires glimmered here and there, surrounded by warriors cooking. The feasting was interrupted only by the revel of the rejoicing. All those Pawnees were mad with delight. They sent their shouts beating up against the night sky.

They were not unheard. In the edge of the trees a solitary warrior looked down on the flames of the fires and the figures of the dancers, leaping up black and tall. He listened to the yells of triumph and his soul swelled high. Stretched along the lower branch of a tree, his horse picketed well behind him in the wood, Thunder Moon stared at the Pawnees and trembled with indignation, like a hungry wolf watching in the distance the banqueting of many coyotes too numerous to be attacked even by his superior might of tooth and shoulder.

He did not have the patience of an Indian, but he had a patience which any white man could have admired. He lay there hour after hour and saw the fires diminish, heard the cries of joy grow fewer, and the screech of horn and whistle die out. Glutted with victory and with boasting, the Pawnees fell asleep. Only here and there a few hardy enthusiasts, chiefly very young men who had not counted a coup before, continued the dancing and the merrymaking. A tall brave hurried up the slope, axe in hand, to bring back wood for the main fire. The spirit of the dance still was upon him and, as he went, he leaped up and down and his whoop went thrilling behind him. Straight under the tree of Thunder Moon he passed. Down upon him dropped a shadow. The Pawnee fell without a sound and there was the heavy, hollow sound of a knife driven home by a strong hand. His medicine bag passed into the possession of the victor and Thunder Moon stood up and laughed down at the noise of the celebration. He laughed silently, for now he could turn back to the far-off village. He had done his deed, counted his coup, and he could return and tell his disheartened people that Spotted Bull was a liar and a fool who made medicine without strength, and who could not give strength to his friends or unnerve his enemies. The proof was the medicine bag of this fallen Pawnee. Yet suppose Spotted Bull declared that the bag must have been picked up from where it lay forgotten on the battlefield?

Thunder Moon lingered on the edge of the woods and passed his tongue across his dry lips. He was athirst with a burning of the soul which cried out for the blood of the Pawnees – and there they were spread out before him, enough to feast even his vengeance. Ah, those wolves of the plains.

The moon rose, hanging a bright, golden disk in the east, and Thunder Moon took it as a token. He went back to the place where he had left his horse and found there his spear, plunged into the ground, and his shield hanging from it. Both these he took and returned with them to the forest's edge. He advanced into the open a few steps and held up shield and spear to the rising moon. It was a dream shield of wonderful power, made in the old days by a forefather of Young Hawk and bequeathed by him to Thunder Moon when the brave died. No bullet struck the warrior who carried that shield in battle! It was round, made of thickened bull's hide, covered with well-dressed antelope skin. Eagle feathers hung from it to signify the flight and power of the king of the sky. It was painted with the mysterious form of the crescent moon, the horns turned upward, and there were four spots to represent the four winds of heaven.

This shield and the long lance Thunder Moon raised to the moon, which now floated in the black bowl of the sky. To the zenith, to the west, he raised them, and last he presented them straight to the moon again and made this prayer aloud:

'White Spirit, look down on me and see me standing here. I am not a stranger to you. My name was taken from your brother, who looks through the thunder clouds. Your image is painted on this magic shield which has covered me in battle so that the arrows, the spears, the bullets, the knives of all my enemies cannot harm me in war. The Sioux, the Comanches, the Crows, the Blackfoot, and the Pawnees know this shield and they know me who carry it. I am Thunder Moon. No man among the Cheyennes is so strong as I. Wherever the plains stretch from the north to the south and from the great river into the western mountains, I am known and I am feared. I know that it is not my strength that conquers but the strength of the Sky People, and chiefly yours. If ever I have sacrificed to you swift horses, and whole buffalo, and beaded suits, and weapons, and painted robes, hear me now! The Pawnee wolves lie by the river, and their bellies are filled with meat. Their brains are more filled with victory over my people who have been fools and trusted to the medicine of a cheat instead of worshipping the Sky People. Now I stand under your white face and wait and watch for a sign to tell me whether I may safely go down among them and come back again, having done things which they will remember. Speak to me, spirit!'

Lance and shield extended above his head stiffly at arm's length, face raised, Thunder Moon waited through long minutes. He seemed to have turned to iron, to be incapable of weariness. At last he said in a low voice, 'My arms fall from my shoulders. My head swims. Speak to me quickly!'

Instantly, as though this message had been heard, a wisp of cloud blew across the disk in the sky, not darkening it but rather absorbing the light and hanging for a moment, like a shining scarf before it vanished. Thunder Moon drew in a great breath. Then, with an effort, he stilled the shout of triumph which trembled in his throat. He turned and hastened back to his horse where he drove the lance into the ground again, hung the sacred shield reverently upon it, – for these weapons would be useless in the work that he intended – and then started straight down the slope for the camp. Even his rifle he had not brought with him, but in the front of his belt was his knife, long bladed, heavy, and strong as a short sword. With a stroke of that knife he had severed the spinal cord of a running buffalo. He carried, moreover, a heavy Colt revolver in a sheath of antelope skin against his thigh, fastened low down, so that it was ready for the quick and practiced touch of his fingers. So equipped he felt that he could give death to seven Pawnees before he died in turn – if the worst came to the worst. The moon shone behind him and he did not fear the brightness of its light. Rather it was a heavenly companion that filled his heart with courage. For had he not prayed and had not his prayer been answered?

He went down the slope hastily. A true Indian of the plains would have moved with less than half his noise, especially through the tall, dried grasses that covered the slope, but his heart was armed with enchanted power, and he was not afraid. He came up to the camp, not crawling but upright, like a man who feels his destiny upon him. Just below the camp was a deep little swale and, as he stepped into it, a form rose before him and held a rifle at his breast.

'What is your name, brother?' asked the Pawnee. 'Have you gone out to give thanks to the night for your dead men?'

'Yes,' said Thunder Moon in the Pawnee tongue which he had learned perfectly from prisoners, 'and you are the second man!'

As he spoke, the knife was conjured into his hand and driven into the heart of the warrior. The latter gave a gasping, half-stifled groan. Thunder Moon, catching the body to keep it from crashing down among the rattling grasses, listened breathlessly. Apparently the groan had not been heard in the Pawnee camp. Only the wind whispered guiltily among the long grasses and, far off, a horse neighed from the opposite side of the sleeping camp.

Thunder Moon, his heart swelling with gratitude and joy, stood erect. He held the limp body of the Pawnee up to the moon and whispered: 'This death and the medicine bag of this warrior, I sacrifice to you, white face!' Then he laid the body softly in the grass, took the medicine bag from about its neck, and walked confidently on into the midst of his enemies.

# 6

# Sleeping Wolves

Most in that camp were sleeping, exhausted by their riding, their battle, and their rejoicings, but many were still awake. Thunder Moon passed within a dozen strides of some of them. However, their eyes were partly blinded by the brightness of their camp fires and partly their suspicions were blinded and could not quite waken at the sight of this tall, naked warrior, striding through the camp.

The prairie sun had bronzed the body of Thunder Moon to a darkness almost as coppery as the color of the true Indian and, by the moonlight, there was nothing to betray him except the length of his hair which flowed far, after the fashion of the Cheyennes. However, he had disguised himself sufficiently in this particular by catching up and putting on one of those wolfish headdresses of which the Pawnees were so fond.

He went straight to the center of the camp where the chiefs should be found. He told himself that, if he could know the face and form of the leader of this brilliant war party, he could strike a blow at the Pawnees which almost at a single stroke would overbalance the whole work of this expedition. He looked down upon an array of scattered warriors, all in the prime of life, magnificent men wrapped in buffalo robes, all fit he thought to lead such an expedition.

Their lances were fixed in the ground. Their shields hung upon them. They seemed to Thunder Moon like silent guardians of the sleepers. Passing man after man, his lips twitched and his fingers tingled for his weapon. How simple it would be to lean and with a stroke of the knife send a spirit wandering on the long road to the sky. But he was not one to strike and count coup while an enemy slept.

He was in the exact center of the camp. Not one of the recumbent forms had stirred. He saw before him what promised to be the goal of his expedition, for here was the long headdress of a chief, decked with eagle feathers hanging from a suspended shield. Two lances were fixed in the ground, side by side. Each supported a shield and from one hung the eagle feathers. On either side of those lances slept a warrior. Which, then, was the wearer of the headdress? Which was the leader of the band? Thunder Moon leaned and stared fixedly at one and then at the other. Both were amazingly young, not far advanced into their twenties. But, after all, fame on the war path did not always accompany age. Youth sometimes would be served even on the blood trail across the plains.

He who seemed the older, and the more likely indeed to be the chief man of the party, lay on the left of the spears. He who seemed the younger lay to their right, which seemed the more suitable position for the chief. Thunder Moon, distracted, looked back to the moon, now sailing high through the black sea of night, putting out the stars as she traveled through the sky. He received no sign to help him in his time of doubt. Close over the younger of the two he leaned and laid the point of his knife on the hollow of the sleeper's throat. Instantly the large eyes opened and looked calmly up into the face of Thunder Moon.

'Pawnee,' he said, speaking that tongue, 'are you not the chief whom all these braves follow?'

The latter looked down at the glittering length of the knife blade. 'I am he!' he replied calmly.

The hand of Thunder Moon tightened on the haft of his weapon, but he could not strike. 'Stand up . . . softly . . . and walk in front of me and out of the camp,' he whispered. 'I walk behind you, and in my hand I have six deaths!' He touched the revolver at his thigh as he spoke. Without a word of protest or argument, the Pawnee rose, softly as he had been bidden.

'If a man stirs, if a man groans,' said Thunder Moon, 'you are dead, Pawnee wolf!'

A loud burst of laughter rolled across to them from the nearest camp fire, where several young braves were seen routing out the sleepers. The heart of Thunder Moon stood still. There was an expectant fear in the eyes of the youthful Pawnee as he glanced at the short gun which was now in the hand of his captor. However, it was not the spreading of an alarm which they had witnessed, merely a fresh outbreak of rejoicing. Soon a dozen braves were capering around the fire and raising hideous war cries.

The prisoner walked straight past the fire and the celebrants toward the edge of the camp, stepping with great care, for his way had to wind back and forth among the sleepers. They were nearly out of the camp when a sleeper wakened suddenly and raised himself upon one elbow. He looked full into the face of the prisoner and raised his hands in a silent salutation. Thunder Moon, making the same salute, followed and felt the keen eyes of the Pawnee looking up at him.

They passed on, but presently Thunder Moon became aware that a man was following – a thing that he judged rather by guess than by sense knowledge for no sound was made by the feet of the trailer, and no shadow was cast by his coming. Yet Thunder Moon knew that there was danger behind him and, turning a little as he wound between two prostrate forms, he risked a backward glance and saw that he who had recently saluted the young chief was now striding erect in his rear.

They passed the edge of the camp and descended into the little swale where Thunder Moon had slain the watcher who had risen out of the tall grass. Just before them and to the left were the horses, totally unguarded. It seemed as though these Pawnees, by the greatness of their victory, felt that they had frightened all danger from the face of the prairies.

'Go toward the horses,' said Thunder Moon to his captive, 'and there pick out a pony and jump on its back and take another horse by the lead rope.'

The ponies wandered here and there, the rawhide lariats trailing behind them. The captive gave no sign but turned toward the horses and went on, tall, slender, lithe, stepping like a cat through the grass so that his footfall made no sound even in its dry and crackling stems.

From behind, equally cat-like, curious, insistent the other Pawnee stalked them without a spoken word. If Thunder Moon turned, the chief before him would whirl about and leap on his shoulders, wielding the short knife which was in his girdle. Or if Thunder Moon attempted first to dispose of the man ahead of him, the rifle which was in the hands of his trailer would instantly be fired into his back. He was in a quandary and, being cornered so deftly by ill chance, he determined to rely upon his spiritual protectors, the Sky People. Up to the ascending moon he raised his eyes and, as he looked down again, he saw his victim step aside and pick up the lead ropes of two ponies. They were admirable specimens of horseflesh. All the followers of the war chief in this raid had been mounted, it appeared, upon specially chosen horses. The sides of these two had been heavily scored with whipstrokes that showed they had been ridden into the battle charge, but otherwise they seemed fresh, and lifted their heads and laid back their ears as the Pawnee approached them.

'Better bad spirit than no spirit at all!' thought Thunder Moon as he regarded those flattened ears.

'Brother,' said a harsh and sudden voice close behind him, 'what Pawnee wears long hair, like a woman or a dog of a Cheyenne?'

What to do then? Thunder Moon, glancing behind him, saw his captive sitting stiffly erect on the back of his pony, obviously ready to whirl and spring to the attack at the first opening. Better the attack of a man armed with a knife than the attack of one who carried a rifle.

'I shall tell you in one word!' said Thunder Moon quietly and, flicking the revolver from his thigh, he only half turned and fired a snap shot under his left arm at the brave behind him. How many hundred times had he practiced that trick, and now his patience was rewarded. The Pawnee had his rifle at the ready with his finger on the trigger. The weapon exploded as he fell with his forehead bored through by that well-aimed ball. The danger hissed close past the head of Thunder Moon, but he had no time to thank the Sky People for that escape from peril. He straightened to meet a shadow flying toward him through the air. The young chief had swung around on the back of his pony and hurled himself like a projectile at his foe. As he leaped, he thrust before him with his knife.

Instinctively Thunder Moon crouched and struck out and up with his left clenched fist. Over his head darted the knife of the Pawnee, a deadly ray of light, and at the same moment his whole arm went numb with the shock of the impact. He felt his knuckles bite through flesh to the bone.

A limp, senseless form struck him, staggered him, and fell inertly upon the ground at his feet, while the terribly loud echoes of the two explosions still rang through the swale with hollow, heavy voices. The camp was already up. Stamp on the ground and every wolf within a mile leaps to his feet. The Pawnees were not less alert than sleeping wolves.

Up to their feet they started, weapons instantly in hand. Their shouts rose in a crash to the trembling moon. The foster son of Big Hard Face stooped to drive his knife into the heart of the fallen Pawnee chief. He saw the young brave lying with his arms thrown above his head, his lips parted, and blood trickling down his cheek from the blow which had stunned him. There was no Cheyenne under the broad heavens who would have hesitated in a similar instance, but Thunder Moon could not strike the decisive blow.

Instead he scooped up the limp body in one powerful arm, caught a frightened pony as it darted past, and threw his burden across its withers. He mounted in turn behind and, with the little beast groaning under the double weight, he forced it to gallop up the slope toward the trees. Like the promise of all blessing, the dark and obscuring shadows of the forest lay before him. As he reached its margin, he looked back and laughed through his teeth. Out from the camp came the first of the Pawnees to sight him as he vanished, but they were well to the rear. His own horse, fresh and strong, waited for him in the midst of the trees. Surely he had more than an even chance to make his escape – aye, and carry his prisoner with him.

# 7

# A Pawnee Brave

He had a triple task before him when he got to his own pony. He had to wrench spear and shield from the ground. He had to tie his prisoner to his own saddle and, leading his warhorse behind him, he had to ride the Pawnee pony on through the trees.

What he would do now, he had determined long before. Beyond the woods lay the broken district of a stretch of badlands and, into that district, undoubtedly the Pawnees would think that he had fled. Whereas on the farther side of the little forest lay the river, and beyond the river there was nothing save the open, moon-lit plains. Yet it was toward them that he headed. As he rode, he heard the hunt crash past toward the hills. He laughed savagely – a laughter that made no sound.

All was well in the heart of Thunder Moon when he reached the edge of the water and saw that no one scouted on the farther bank. He rode boldly in, heedless in such a moment of a proper ford. At once the strong current foamed around the two swimming horses. They began to whirl around and around, their brave, pricked ears flattened, a sure sign of desperation in them. Thunder Moon was about to strike out for himself toward the farther bank when they hit a shallow sand bank and, in another moment, were climbing the farther shore.

The captive, dazed, choking, coughing forth water from his lungs, had been brought back to his wits by that involuntary bath. Almost at once he whirled about as far as the rope permitted him to move in order to see in what manner he could annoy his captor. He looked down along the great war spear of Thunder Moon, its narrow head glistening like eyes of vengeance.

'If you cry out, friend,' said Thunder Moon gravely, 'I strike this spear through your heart and choke the noise you try to make.'

The Pawnee stared at the spear point as though bewitched, and made no response. At length he murmured: 'Tarawa has bewitched my brothers. He has veiled their eyes. Lo, there they ride. I see their shadows sweeping along the river and across the hills, and yet they will not look down and see me here.'

'Friend,' answered Thunder Moon with satisfaction, 'the eyes see only what the brain wishes them to know.'

'It is true,' groaned the young Pawnee. 'My brothers ride toward the hills to find me, never dreaming that you would dare to come by this open way. You know it so well,' he added, turning to Thunder Moon with wonder, 'that you will not even gallop the horses.'

'If we rode fast, we would make a streak across the plain,' Thunder Moon explained. 'The moonlight would glance on us. We would be discovered. Now we journey slowly, and the moon mist swallows us. We are no more than ghosts to them already.'

He laughed, but this time he allowed his voice to make a little sound. It rumbled deeply in his throat, like an ominous music.

It seemed the captive saw that all hope was lost for him. He breathed deeply, as though about to utter the war cry which would send the spear of his captor through his heart but which also might doom his slayer to quick vengeance at the hands of the pursuing Pawnees. Yet, as the cry formed in his throat and at his lips, he looked again at the ready spear of Thunder Moon and checked the shout. To the young, hope is a giant!

So they rode on and, finally, all sights and sounds of the camp were lost behind them. The night grew older still. The wide silence of the plains received them and in turn the cold gray of the dawn began to be sketched across the eastern horizon.

They reached a little rivulet, running not a hundred yards from its fountain head before it sank into the thirsty prairie again. Here Thunder Moon looked to his captive, washed the blood from the wound which his knuckles had made in the cheek of the Pawnee, and then freed him from the cruel strands of the rope.

'There is a long trail before us,' said Thunder Moon. 'Let us ride like friends. I have no pleasure in tormenting you. All the while, I shall watch you. The little gun in my hand . . . you have seen that it does not strike in vain. So be warned, my friend.'

The Pawnee said nothing for some time after this. He kept his head high, yet it was plain that rage, shame, and despair were at work in him. He held his glance straight before him and his jaw was set.

At length, Thunder Moon stopped to break his fast. He was no patient endurer of long famines. He had knocked down two rabbits with expert shots of his revolver and paused to make a fire and cook the game. The eyes of the Pawnee stared first at his captor, and then were slowly raised to follow the gradually ascending smoke which climbed the great arch of the sky.

Thunder Moon understood that surprised glance, but he said nothing. Only when the rabbits were cooked, did he offer one of them, neatly browned on a wooden spit, to the other.

The Pawnee stared again. 'My friend,' he said in a pleasant and surprisingly gentle voice, 'in the towns of the Cheyennes I know that the Pawnees are dogs and the sons of dogs. They are hated and they are feared. One Pawnee scalp is more prized than five scalps of the Sioux or even more than a Comanche's. Yet . . . one does not stop to cook in the open prairie when there may be danger on the trail . . . or offer food to a dog. Is it true?'

'I am too hungry to think clearly,' Thunder Moon said frankly. 'You are hungry, also. Eat, my friend.'

So they ate together and, from time to time, Thunder Moon observed his captive. The longer he regarded him, the more certain he was that this was indeed the war chief for, even if the brave had not confessed his identity, there was about him such an air of dignity and grace as Thunder Moon never before had seen – not among the tall Cheyennes, not among the well-made Crows or the graceful Blackfoots. The Pawnees tended to a broad and heavy build as a rule. This warrior was shaped with infinite skill, and his face, too, varied from the usual appearance of an Indian. It was more oval. The eyes were larger and set in under a deep and thoughtful brow. His features were molded with the same beauty and regularity with which his body was formed. This Pawnee was such a man Thunder Moon felt fear never could come near him, simply because fear was an ungraceful passion and unworthy of such a creature.

'Noble brother,' said Thunder Moon at last, 'I have heard the great chiefs of your nation named. Some of them I have met in battle, and I have seen them charge along the lines of the Cheyennes. I have not seen you. You are a stranger to me. Yet a tree does not grow from a slip to a great height in one day, and a man does not become great suddenly. Never have the Cheyennes been struck a blow as you struck them yesterday. Tell me, where have you hidden yourself that you have not appeared before this upon the plains? It is well for the Cheyennes that the fire is ended before it had a chance to consume them.'

The eyes of the captive glistened. 'It is well!' he said.

'Why do you call it well?' asked Thunder Moon naively. 'Is it well that you should be here with me, journeying where I am to take you?'

'Where I go,' said the Pawnee, 'is a small thing. Where I travel, the Pawnees will hardly care. Only one man among them will yearn for me greatly.'

Thunder Moon stared.

'I have spoken!' ended the other.

'You have spoken strangely,' declared Thunder Moon. 'Are the Pawnees worse than wolves in winter who eat their dead? Do they forget their great men as soon as they have fallen?'

'No,' said the youth, 'but I have done no great deeds. If I have counted seven coups ... why, that is not many. If I have slain four men in battle, that also is not much. It is well that all the four were Cheyennes. Their spirits are lost between earth and heaven. Their scalps will hang in my lodge and dry there in the smoke. Their medicine bags and their souls in them shall be sacrificed to Tarawa.'

Thunder Moon fondled the haft of his long knife with a loving touch and, at the same time, regarded the other with a melancholy eye.

'Look, my friend,' he said, 'you walk now on a dangerous trail. Still I listen. Your words I cannot altogether understand. That man who led the Pawnees in the battle of yesterday is no unskillful warrior. What if no more than four men have fallen behind his hand? The brain is mightier than the arm, both in council and in battle. Though he never strikes a single blow himself, he would have caused the death of hundreds of the enemies of his people if he had lived. If he had lived!' added Thunder Moon, and dwelt upon the Pawnee with an infinite satisfaction.

However, the latter seemed not a whit dismayed. He even laughed a little, softly and deeply in his throat, as a man will do when he exults greatly. 'He lives and the hundreds of whom you speak shall fail. He will wash the prairies with blood, even for my sake.'

'For your sake?' echoed Thunder Moon.

'For my sake, Cheyenne! Because I told you that I was the leader when you leaned above me, your knife at my throat, does it follow that I am in fact the chief?'

Thunder Moon was silent, watching with burning eyes. Truth and ecstasy of great accomplishment were stamped upon the face and trembling in the voice of the Pawnee.

'For if I had denied it, your knife would have turned from me and entered the heart of the son of my father!'

'The son of your father?'

'Falling Stone! Falling Stone is my brother and our leader. It was he who washed his hands in the blood of the best of the Cheyennes yesterday. He still lives, and he shall not die until he has swept the Cheyennes howling from the plains and driven them into the Father of Waters. I have spoken! Open the sky, and Tawara strike me if I have not told the truth . . . if I have not made a prophecy.'

# 8

# Matching Wits

Very great had been the hopes which Thunder Moon had founded upon that midnight exploit of his. Now he found his hopes dashed quite to the ground. His heart welled in him with disappointment first, and then with a deadly rage against his companion.

'Traitor . . . dog of a Pawnee!' he gasped.

He lurched a little forward and caught the shoulder of the youth in that terrible clasp which the strongest men of the Cheyennes knew so well and feared so much – that grip which, as men said, in the midst of battle when all other weapons were broken or lost had served him to tear the life out of a foeman as you or I might pluck out the core from an orange.

The Pawnee endured that grip, though the iron finger tips were biting through his flesh and grinding the nerves against the bone. He endured it and, although the sweat started upon his forehead, he smiled calmly, proudly, even disdainfully upon Thunder Moon.

'Strike when you will, friend,' said the Pawnee. 'I have told you the truth. That is a snake which only bites the heel of a villain. And I have seen you stung.'

It was on the whole as well-rounded an insult as could have been flung in the face of a Cheyenne, and Thunder Moon gasped deeply with fury. Twice the long blade of his hunting knife gleamed naked of the sheath, and twice he thrust it back within the leather. At last he sat back, frowning.

'You see the torture before you,' he said, 'and you see the Chey-enne women . . . whose fathers and brothers and sons have fallen by your hand and by the weapons of your men . . . you see them gathered around you, tearing your flesh, burning you, filling your ears with taunts, dangling before your face your own scalp. Therefore, the greater the chief the greater the torment. So you would belie yourself, discard your name, and take another. That is the game of a child, and I smile at you, and understand the trick.'

'You lie,' replied the Pawnee, with a sneer. 'As I hang on the stake, I shall laugh at the Cheyenne she-devils as they tear me. I shall laugh when my own scalp is dangled in my face. Until death chokes me, I shall shout out the names of the Cheyenne warriors who have fallen under my hand. I shall laugh and sing my battle song and my death song, and make my boast true in the ears of men and in the ears of Tarawa who hears all things.' He looked up, and smiled at the sun-flooded sky.

Thunder Moon listened aghast, for now he felt that he had heard the truth, indeed. So this great exploit, this greatest of his deeds, was a useless thing. He sighed bitterly. 'I have asked too much,' he said. 'The Sky People heard only a part of my prayer.'

'Brother,' said the Pawnee with the same disdainful smile, 'did you think that the Sky People to whom you prayed could have filled your hands with such glory as the death of Falling Stone? No, he is a war-rior who is not fated to die in such manner. When he falls, thousands shall fall around him. Wait but a little and you shall have a sign from him. For he comes across the prairies swifter than a great fire, scourged along by the wind. The horses die under him as he rides. He sings a terrible song in his heart: "My brother, Rising Cloud, is lost to me! A thousand men shall die for his sake!" '

As he spoke, he swept his hand toward the horizon, and Thunder Moon, so had the words worked upon him, started a little and bit his lip when he saw that he had shown his emotion. For that matter, he never had been able to control his expression with the true immobil-ity of feature that distinguishes an Indian of pure blood.

'Words are not bullets,' said Thunder Moon dryly, 'and speeches are not armed warriors charging together. It may be that some day I shall meet this Falling Stone, this brother, and there shall be mourning in the lodge of your father and your mother again. There are some who reap glory and gather it like corn, and preserve it like pemmican. Others take what has been reaped and what has been preserved and it is they who eat it. But you, Rising Cloud, you are young, and yet you are very brave.'

The Pawnee was so amazed by this compliment that he was utterly speechless for a long moment.

'You are brave,' said Thunder Moon, speaking his thoughts aloud, rather than addressing his prisoner directly, 'and you are wise as well. You were wise in what you said to me. What courage is greater than for a man to die for another . . . even for his brother?' He paused.

'A thought comes to me,' continued Thunder Moon. 'It may be that you will not die under the hands of the squaws and the children while the Cheyenne braves look on. I have promised a sacrifice to the Sky People who brought me safely into the camp of Falling Stone and took me out again. It might be, Rising Cloud, that you would be a sacrifice acceptable to them. I would not sacrifice a scalped and dishonored man. How could a wandering ghost be acceptable to them? One who had lost his medicine bag and his soul? One who could not ride on the plains above us and follow the buffalo over the shadows in the sky? So I have this thought, Rising Cloud, of dressing you in all the regalia of a great Pawnee chief and then striking you dead as an offering to the Sky People. After that, I would bury you honorably, and kill a fine horse beneath the frame on which your body lay, and put weapons beside you, even good rifles and knives, and all that a spirit could need in the hereafter.'

When he had finished this singular speech, Rising Cloud maintained an erect head for a moment only, and then his glance dropped to the ground. In this manner they remained for some time, the foster son of the Cheyenne turning his thought in his mind and finding it good, and the Pawnee apparently overcome by this generous offer. A death by indescribable torment had lain before him. To avoid it, he had badgered this pale-skinned enemy in the hope of provoking a sudden thrust of the knife. Now, however, he was promised an end almost as honorable as death in the midst of battle, charging at the side of one's best friends for the honor of the tribe.

'How many,' asked the Pawnee suddenly, 'died in the camp of my brother last night? From how many did you take the medicine bags?'

'Three,' said Thunder Moon, and went on with his secret thoughts calmly.

'Three men died under your hand, and a fourth was carried away a prisoner like a child or a helpless woman!' said the Pawnee, writhing with shame. 'It is plain,' he added, raising his head again, 'that the Sky People gave you power. Tarawa willed it. He would not have the Pawnees too proud. He wished to tame the high spirit of Falling Stone after the great victory. So he chose the hand of Thunder Moon, who is the heart and the head and the hand of the Cheyennes.'

At this, the big man looked up sharply. 'How did you know my name, brother?' he asked.

'The wolf kills in one way,' said the Pawnee, 'and the mountain lion does not have two ways of killing the deer. Have I not heard the story of how a Cheyenne rode far south to the camp of the Comanches and killed in that camp and brought away the greatest medicine of the tribe?'

'So!' breathed Thunder Moon, 'that is known even to the Pawnees.'

'Besides,' said the young chief, and he smiled a little, 'I have not heard that there are two Cheyennes with pale faces and with hands of iron. We know you, brother. When I looked up from my sleep and saw the glittering of your knife, had it been any other man, I should have struck one blow for my life and to alarm the camp. But I saw that it was Thunder Moon, and I gave up hope.'

The delicious sweetness of praise ran softly and kindly into the soul of Thunder Moon, but he controlled himself and said merely: 'It is time that we take the trail once more.'

So they mounted and resumed their way across the plains, refreshed. They continued through the day, goading the sides of their weary horses. The hot sun dipped into the western haze. It set and the day was covered with delicate color. Immediately afterwards, they could see dim lights twinkling before them and, coming closer, they saw the Cheyenne village spread out before them.

It was always a noisy time of the day for it was the moment when the boys, bringing in the horses which they had herded and guarded during the day, swept with whoops and yells into the camp. It was the time, too, when the braves went forth often and shouted their invitations to a feast. There was the neighing of horses and their frightened snorting as they were tethered for the night nearby. Now, however, all these sounds were lacking. But first, from the distance, it seemed that one long, shrill voice was wailing out of the edge of the sky and, as the two drew closer, they heard this sound dissolved into many portions. Each was the lament of a woman, sharp and thin, and reaching over the prairie as far as the cry of a hunting wolf.

'You hear?' said Thunder Moon grimly. 'It is a token that Falling Stone is not forgotten in the village of the Suhtai. When you enter that place with me, you ride into great danger, my brother. Yet keep a strong heart. I shall not forsake you. Ride before me. Go slowly and yet never stop, even if a crowd gathers close before your horse. Ride straight into the center of the village, and when you see a bear lodge, with a great red bear painted along the side of it with wonderful art, you will know that that is the home of my father, Big Hard Face. Go to that lodge and dismount. I shall be close behind you, protecting you.'

'It is well,' said the Pawnee. 'Yet,' he added wistfully, 'if you will sacrifice me to the Sky People who are your friends, Tarawa who hears all things and sees all things is as near to me now as he will be in the center of the Cheyenne camp. Strike now, Thunder Moon, and accomplish your vow for, if you take me into the village, the women who have lost husbands and sons in the battle will tear me out of your hands. I have seen such things happen. I know them very well.'

'Brother,' said Thunder Moon calmly, 'I am not a young man. Among the Cheyennes my name is known. I do not take you in among my people in order to shame you or put you in danger at the devilish hands of the women. There is another purpose which you serve in coming with me into the camp of the Cheyennes. I have to prove that one man there is a liar. After that is done, have no fear. You shall die simply and quickly.'

'It is well,' repeated the Pawnee.

42

# 9

# Thunder Moon's Return

At the edge of the village the wailing of the women had increased in volume and had become wildly poignant cries, each with its separate, hoarse note of woe. There Thunder Moon paused and, taking his robe from his own shoulders, he threw it around those of his companion.

'Because,' he said, 'it is not good that a great man and a chief should be naked before the eyes of strangers.'

Rising Cloud gave his captor a single glance brimming and brilliant with gratitude, and then they entered the camp. They had made no other preparation, except that Thunder Moon had tied to his lance, near its point, the three medicine bags which he had taken from his victims in the Pawnee camp. These dangled – strange small shapes – one the tiny skin of a field mouse, one the pelt of a small muskrat, and one was the soft hide of a chipmunk. In them were who could tell what odd trinkets, the collection of which had been commanded by the same dreams that made the warriors who had owned these bags in the first place go out to collect them. There was about them, in spite of their small size and their strange appearance, a mysterious importance, at least in the eyes of all who knew their significance. For they were, almost literally, the souls of men – the souls of dead men, still lingering upon the earth in this form. No matter how bravely the hero might have died, no matter with what perfect ceremonies he were buried, still because he had lost his medicine bag, all peace was stolen from his spirit forever.

There was such excitement through the village that no attention was paid to the two horsemen, for they were only now and again illumined by the light from within a lodge whose flap hung open.

They had covered almost half the distance to the center of the village when the harsh, crackling voice of an old man sang out: 'The medicine of Spotted Bull lied when it said that Thunder Moon would not return to the Suhtai. It lied, for here is Thunder Moon, and he brings a companion with him.'

Straight before them at that moment was a woman seated in the middle of the way, cross-legged, covered with dirt. Her long hair she had shorn away with slashes of a knife and some of those cuts had gashed her scalp and let the blood flow. Furthermore, she had slashed her legs and arms and breasts with the same knife which she still brandished in her hand and which she sometimes waved over her head, all the while keeping up a terrible keening. Often it was a wordless lament. Again, it took shape in words: 'Sky People, under earth spirits, spirits that live in the water, how did Big River hurt you? When was he not your friend? You deserted him. You went from him. Then you held his arms so that he could not strike the Pawnee wolf who came and tore at his breast. Yet his heart was great. He would not die even from such a terrible wound. He kept fighting. You wanted to have him dead. You held his arms, and two more Pawnee devils leaped on him and bore him down. He lies far off on the plains. The river has rolled him ashore like a dead pebble. His body is filled with water. The medicine bag is gone from his throat. His scalp drips blood from the bridle of a Pawnee. And I am here! Pity me! Take my life from me quickly! Carry me away to Big River. There let my soul dwindle and fade from the earth with his soul, until both become so thin that even the eye of Tarawa cannot see us. Let me die. I do not wish to live. I have a brother and a sister who will take care of my son. Let me die. I ask you for death. I am sad and sick of living, and my teepee is empty. Oh, my lodge is empty and the pipe that hangs from the lodge pole never will be smoked again.'

In this manner she lamented, and all these exclamations were interspersed with wild, long-drawn, animal-like cries and howls, and then heartbroken sobbings. When she heard the name of Thunder Moon, it startled her to her feet. Up she bounded, knife in hand, and throwing herself down before the warrior she literally embraced the knees of his tired pony – which, except for its weariness, would have trampled her into the ground.

'I cried out!' she screamed up to the brave. 'I cried out, and the spirits heard me, and they sent me Thunder Moon. Oh, Thunder Moon, Spotted Bull lied when he said that you would not return to us. He lied, too, when he sent our braves out and would not let you lead them. May he die . . . may he rot like mildewed meat! For if you had led our warriors, they never would have been beaten. No, they would be riding back now with scalps at their bridles. They would be dancing around the fires, counting their coups. Oh, may Spotted Bull shrivel away like grass in the first heats. May he. . . .'

Here two other women rushed to her and tried to cover her mouth with their hands, cautioning her, begging her not to bring her soul into mortal peril by challenging the wrath of the medicine man.

'He dares not touch me, the liar and cheat, the mangy dog, Spotted Bull. For Thunder Moon is here. To my husband he was a brother. When Thunder Moon and Big River rode out together, they made the Pawnees tremble. Spotted Bull separated them and therefore let him die and be shamed before all men and let. . . .' She broke off and added: 'Thunder Moon, Thunder Moon, my husband's friend, be a friend to me.'

'I am your friend,' said the warrior gently.

'Then go to the river, find his body. Take me to find his body and bury it. The same water that took his dead body, let it take my dead one, and so my soul shall float down the stream and come to his soul.'

Before an answer could be given, through the crowd which had begun to gather a loud voice sounded: 'Who is the fool who curses Spotted Bull and wishes for his death? Who is she?' Spotted Bull himself came striding through the crowd, who gave way before him.

He came directly to the squaw of Big River and she cringed away from him, taking shelter between her two companions. Even these two seemed quite anxious to get away from her, and tried vainly to disengage the hands with which she clutched them so firmly.

'The going of Big River may have been only a token and a sign,' said Spotted Bull, extending his clenched hand over the squaw. 'Bring two good horses and tie them to the post in front of my lodge. It may be that I may be able to intercede with the Sky People and turn their anger away from you because you have cursed me. Unless. . . .'

Hundreds had gathered and still were gathering. The space between the teepees was jammed tight with men and women and children, so that the Pawnee, trying to get ahead through the mob, found himself lodged there and helpless, unable to move.

Here the stern voice of Thunder Moon broke in. 'Spotted Bull, spotted calf, spotted coyote, take your hand from the woman. I have come back to let the Cheyennes know that you are a liar and a fool! Do not look at the squaw of Big River whom you sent out to death with the other warriors. Look to me. You gave them weak medicine. You put a curse on me. Your medicine was nothing. The Sky People laughed at you. Here are medicine bags of the Pawnees to prove that I have been among them.'

Spotted Bull, who had stormed up to the squaw in such a passion that he had been blind to all other faces and forms, now looked up to the towering silhouette of the man on horseback. At that instant the flap of an adjoining teepee was thrown open and a flickering, wild firelight streamed out upon the face of Thunder Moon. So Spotted Bull went backwards a step, staggering like one who has received a heavy blow. A sort of groan of interest and of fear came from the lips of the crowd. It was a terrible thing to which they had listened – never before in the annals of the Suhtai had a chief medicine man been denounced in the face of the entire tribe in this fashion. He recovered himself almost at once, for he was one who made his living as an actor and by the constant use of words. He called out, pointing to the medicine bags which dangled from the head of the war spear of the brave:

'After the bear has fought and feasted, the buzzards steal down from the sky and eat also. You have sneaked up onto the battlefield. You have found dead Pawnees and stolen their medicine bags before their friends could bury them. You come here and talk loudly, but men know that every liar has a huge voice.'

There was another gasp from the crowd. They seemed to think that the spear of Thunder Moon would be buried in the breast of the medicine man the next instant. So, doubtless, it would have been, had Spotted Bull carried a gun or even a knife. As it was, he stood defenseless before the warrior, showing such courage as few men in the tribe would have exhibited at such a moment.

'I have not come back here to murder you, Spotted Bull,' said Thunder Moon. 'I have come back to kill your reputation. I shall make you laughed at even by the children. Your own squaws will scorn you and spit on you. Do you say that I have not been in the camp of the Pawnees?'

'I say it and I know it,' went on the medicine man, boldly brazening out the situation, for he saw that either he or Thunder Moon must go down on this occasion.

'By your medicine you know it?' asked Thunder Moon in a dry voice.

There was not so much as the whispering sound of a drawn breath through all the crowd. Never before had they come to a moment of such terrible interest. For no warrior in their tribe was so great as Thunder Moon. No medicine man had such a reputation as Spotted Bull. How often his medicine had brought rain. How often his medicine had sent them out to successful battle or to good hunting. It was now the meeting of flesh and spirit. And great things were expected.

'Yes,' said the medicine man, 'I talked to the spirits. A spirit came like an owl and sat on my shoulder and told me that you had crept out onto the battlefield and tried to steal a great name by taking these three medicine bags.'

'Hear me, Spotted Bull,' said Thunder Moon. 'Do you know the name of the chief of the Pawnees who led the army?'

'It is Falling Stone. The spirits have told me. They told me after the braves started on the trail. I tried to call them back to tell them that the Sky People had given luck to the Pawnees. All that happened was revealed to me . . . and that included your wretched treachery.'

'That is not true!' shrilled the sudden voice of the squaw of Big River. 'When has Thunder Moon lied in all his life?'

# 10

# A Warrior Waits

'Woman,' cried the medicine man to the squaw, 'because you made your husband sin, he died. Now you draw down on your head the. . . .'

'Harken to me, Spotted Bull,' broke in Thunder Moon. 'You have told me the name of the chief of the Pawnees. Have the spirits told you the name of his brother, also?'

'What is that? I ask only for the chief leader,' replied the medicine man.

'I shall tell you the name of Falling Stone's brother. Do you wish to know?'

Spotted Bull stretched out his long arm and shook his finger toward Thunder Moon. 'Hear this man, oh my brothers!' he cried. 'With the heart and the soul of a liar, he is striving to turn your minds to other things . . . small things . . . while he juggles his words and makes small matters into great ones, so that you may forget him and his lies!'

'I shall tell you,' said Thunder Moon, 'that the brother of the war chief of the Pawnees also is a great warrior. The scalps of the Cheyennes dry now in his tent. His name is Rising Cloud.'

'More lies!' said the medicine man. 'I smell them afar like a carrion which has lain a fortnight on the ground and in the sun. More lies!'

'They are truths,' answered Thunder Moon. 'Now I shall shut your mouth forever, Spotted Bull, and make you less than a starved dog in this camp, less than a toothless old dog that no longer can crack a bone. Do you hear me? Do you hear me, all my friends of the Suhtai? There sits Rising Cloud on that horse, wrapped in his robe. The medicine of Spotted Bull was fool's medicine. He sent out your young men to their death. But, in spite of him, I went behind the war party. I came up and saw them fleeing from the river. Then I crossed the river and went into the woods that stood on the hills near the camp of the Pawnees. I was so close that their howling over the victory filled my ears. Then I went down into their camp to get their best man, their leader. By chance I missed him. The moon spirit and the Sky People helped me and brought me to the right place, but there like a blind man I failed to see the war chief. I brought away a brave warrior, his brother, as a proof that Spotted Bull is a fool and a coward, and that his medicine is weaker than water.'

As though to verify what had been said, at this moment Rising Cloud allowed the robe to fall away from his head and the familiar headdress of a Pawnee was instantly recognized. A wail of wonder and delight went up from all in the crowd and that wail, like a roaring voice of fate, silenced Spotted Bull.

He shrank back, scowling and muttering. As others pressed forward, he allowed himself to drift toward the rear, and presently disappeared, to skulk softly away toward his own lodge. There he sat with his robe gathered about his head, speaking not at all, while his frightened wives moved like shadows here and talked with one another by the sign language.

However, now that the mass of listening, excited Cheyennes stirred before them, Thunder Moon pressed ahead, and carried the young prisoner with him. They managed to make their way only with great difficulty. The warriors were sullen and silent for the most part as they saw the prisoner go past them. The younger men and boys screamed with pleasure and almost forgot the greatness of the defeat in this sight. But the danger was from the women who had lost kin in the battle.

Knives flashed and clubs were swung up on either hand, and many a deadly blow would have been directed at the Pawnee if it had not been for the thundering voice of his captor, following rapidly in the rear and calling to the Suhtai women to beware.

'If there is harm done to the Pawnee,' Thunder Moon shouted, 'I shall take vengeance for it, blood for blood, and head for head! Beware and keep back. The Sky People have sent him to us. Let us treat him as a gift from heaven.'

Thus calling out, he managed to keep Rising Cloud from harm. They pressed on through a growing pandemonium until they came to the central portion of the village, and there reached the lodge of Big Hard Face, with the walking bear painted in brilliant red upon it.

The old man was standing at the flap of the teepee, his arms folded inside his robe. It fitted neither his position nor his age to rush away and mingle with the curious to learn the news, but his eyes were flashing. For he had heard the name of Thunder Moon shouted, and he could not tell in what connection – whether it meant news of life or news of death – until he saw the familiar great shoulders of the rider breaking through the mass with the Pawnee herded before him.

He started violently and raised a hand in salutation. He permitted himself no word of triumph or of exultation, merely gathering his arms again inside his robe, while his foster son dismounted. Indeed, whether emotion had mastered him or he wished to appear indifferent, he turned and disappeared into the teepee, where his son and the prisoner immediately followed him.

Only White Crow remained outside the lodge. All the life of Thunder Moon, since first he had been brought, a crying infant, to the lodge of Big Hard Face, White Crow had been divided between interest and pride on the one hand, and aversion on the other. This was no child of her childless body; neither was it a child of her nephew, Big Hard Face. Therefore, she detested Thunder Moon and all the ways in which his white blood appeared. On that score she never ceased badgering the chief about his foster son. On the other hand, her breast swelled with joy and pride because of the exploits of this young warrior who rode out from her teepee. She remained outside the lodge, boasting in a loud, shrill voice, taunting her neighbors by name.

'Who has gone out from your lodge, Wind Woman, and brought back glory and prisoners? Red Leaf, who is it that has gone out from your lodge and done such things? I send out Thunder Moon. A great, bright moon that blinds the eyes of the Pawnees. Like a thunderstorm he strikes them down. They shrink before him. He leans from his horse and picks up their chief men and brings them back with him like antelope meat.' In this manner she boasted.

Presently the head men of the Suhtai began to arrive at the teepee and, one by one, they passed inside the home of their old chief. Excitement waxed constantly in the gathering crowd. There the women who mourned for dead kinsmen had drawn to the front covered with blood from the gashes which they had inflicted upon one another. Their clothes in rent rags, their bodies covered with dust and with ashes, now they had forgotten their laments and with one voice they demanded that the prisoner be led forth and delivered over into their hands. He was their due. They had earned the right to send his soul on the long journey with all the cunning torments which their hands could devise. They shouted, and the shrill voice of White Crow boasted, as she walked back and forth in front of the teepee.

Inside, there was another scene. Guarded by two famous warriors, the prisoner sat cross-legged at one side. His face was utterly immobile, his fine eyes apparently unconscious of the keen, cruel glances which were fixed upon him, and his ears apparently unaware of the debate which raged concerning him.

First of all, as was his duty, but with perfect simplicity and without boasting, Thunder Moon told a straightforward tale of how he had approached the Pawnee camp, watched it, listened to the songs and shoutings of his enemy, and then made his prayer to the Sky People and his guardian spirit in the moon. How he had struck down the forager for wood. How he had gone into the camp and killed a warrior on the way. How he had gained the central place and found the insignia of the chief. How he had taken the wrong man, as it appeared. How he had led him out and been followed by a suspicious Pawnee. How he had killed this man also, and how he had finally escaped almost by miracle from the swarming Pawnee hunters who rode to find him. Here, then, was the prisoner. For his part, he had a mind to lead out the chief at the next moon rise and sacrifice him in return for the aid which the Sky People had given to him. This was a matter in which the wise men of the tribe should first be consulted.

The old chief had the right of first speech. He shook his head and bade others offer their opinions.

Snake-That-Talks – a young man but a famous fighter, and long ago a companion of Thunder Moon on that famous war trail which carried him first deep into the country of the Comanches – was the first to speak. He said: 'A scalp is a scalp and a coup is good to count. Besides, the women deserve to have sport with this man. More than this, it will gladden the spirits of many unhappy Cheyennes who now are wandering spirits, drifting here and there about that river where they died. It will gladden them to see a Pawnee ghost come so quickly to join them! Let Rising Cloud be given to the women . . . only let Thunder Moon count coup upon him three times and take his scalp when the women have ended their pleasure with him.'

Thunder Moon, listening, leaned forward and looked intently into the face of the captive, but the latter gave no sign that he had heard this terrible advice. Most of the others agreed to this scheme, except Gray Eagle, who declared that some good might be done the tribe by trading the prisoner back to the Pawnees because the war chief, Falling Stone, doubtless would pay an enormous price to redeem his brother.

'Brother,' said Big Hard Face at this point, 'all the horses and all the buffalo on the plains could not pay for all the men we have lost. Our young men, too, will grow afraid of the Pawnees after this battle unless they see a fresh scalp before long. Give us Rising Cloud, my son. Let us do what we will with him. Let the women have him, saving only his scalp for you.'

Twice Thunder Moon attempted to speak and twice his voice failed him. He could not withdraw his eyes from the handsome, immobile face of his captive. At length he said: 'This is not a little thing. I have promised a great sacrifice to the Sky People. Let me have until tomorrow to think about this thing. As for the women,' he added with a sudden flash of disgust, 'they yell like coyotes. Let them wait. I shall tell them my thoughts later.'

# Dangerous Gifts

It is necessary to go back to the raid of the Pawnees to describe a most important detail that now had bearing upon the course of events. When Falling Stone and his band swept down upon the Cheyenne village, they carried away with them a great portion of the horses of the Suhtai. They even made some lucky inroads upon the band of Thunder Moon's Comanche ponies. But the tribe also underwent a loss more mortal than that of men or ponies.

Long ago, when Big Hard Face came back from his foray carrying his white foster son in his arms, he was riding upon a tall dark chestnut stallion, taken from a breeder of Thoroughbreds, with blood as pure and an ancestry more ancient than the blood of kings. That great horse became the father of a line of such stock as the plains Indians had never ridden before. Hardy as the Indian ponies, but with galloping powers far beyond the stretch of any known pony's legs, the chestnuts had served as mounts for Thunder Moon's band on that famous occasion when he foraged deep in the territory of the Comanches and had scoured away from all pursuit.

Upon one of those chestnuts, therefore, he would have been mounted at the time of the Pawnee foray had it not been that those chosen animals had been put out to graze under careful guard at a distance from the camp. There they were safe enough, it seemed. Trained and schooled more carefully than the Indian children themselves, these horses came at a whistle and obeyed the voice almost as though they understood human speech. Therefore, they could not be stampeded. On two occasions when skillful thieves had managed to get on the back of one of Big Hard Face's chestnuts, the faithful animals had come back to the call of their master and brought their would-be captors with them. So it was considered safe enough to range the horses at a distance from the camp, under a guard of three or four men, keeping them always where the choicest grass was to be found.

On the very night when Thunder Moon returned with his prisoner, disastrous tidings were brought in that the impossible had been accomplished. Five of the chestnuts had been taken in the dusk of that same day, taken by a sort of magic and spirited away from the hollow in which they were grazing. The guards made only a feeble effort to follow the trail when they noticed the loss. Darkness closed on the prairie. So they came back to report the loss.

Five out of twelve magnificent horses were gone, and the guards dared not go directly to Big Hard Face, but came and touched the feet of Thunder Moon as he lay asleep. To him they told their story and he in turn took heart and reported the tragedy to his father. There had been no sign of any danger on the plains, the herdsmen reported. Only, in the late afternoon, a great buffalo wolf had been observed sitting on the top of a distant hummock.

Straightway Big Hard Face, Thunder Moon, and half a dozen of the best trailers in the tribe made ready to mount the remaining chestnuts and start the pursuit. They made their preparations with heavy hearts. They were far behind. The dark had passed and the dawn had come since the thief made off with his prizes. Scarcely ten days of hard riding could make up for the difference, even with the best of luck.

While the preparations for departure were underway, an event happened which filled the mind of Thunder Moon with something other than troubles about horseflesh. Already in the rosy light of the morning, the squaws were beginning their keening at a distance from the camp, and the melancholy sounds came from afar in the saddest of music when Thunder Moon, standing in front of his foster father's lodge, heard a tumult down the main passage through the teepees and presently he saw the Omissis, Walking Horse, riding toward him.

A little crowd was running out to look at the chief, then hastily gathering around behind him. It seemed to Thunder Moon that their attention was not so much fixed upon the Omissis as upon something behind him. A little later he could see that a woman followed the chief. As the pair drew closer, he could see that it was such a woman as never before had entered the Suhtai camp.

For she had long, red hair and even from a distance it flashed like two copper swords, curving down from her brows and over her shoulders in massive braids. Her skin was not so swarthy as that of an Indian belle, but was a rich, dark olive. Though she was not tall, she carried herself in such a manner that she filled the eyes entirely. Thunder Moon never had seen a creature quite like her in all the days of his life.

In the meantime, the Omissis came to the lodge entrance and saluted Thunder Moon and Big Hard Face, who had just come out.

'Brothers,' he said, smiling upon them, 'I have come back, and I have brought the payment for the fifty horses as we planned and bargained together.' So saying, he pointed to a whole string of pack ponies now approaching, driven forward by several of Walking Horse's tribesmen. The arrival of such a cargo put off even the thoughts of redeeming the five lost chestnuts.

The pack ponies came up and, one by one, they were unloaded of such treasure as rarely had come under the eye of an Indian in one bulk. There were nearly a hundred rifles. There were quantities of powder and lead. There were five six-shooters of the new Colt pattern – miracle guns they seemed to the Cheyennes, even though they had watched them at work in the hands of Thunder Moon. His shooting with them was considered rather as 'medicine' than as his able use of a weapon. Besides, there were plaited robes and beaded suits, and excellent knives and, indeed, all that could gladden the heart of a Suhtai. In heaps this treasure was carried into the lodge of Big Hard Face, and White Crow received it, gloating over its masses.

'We are to take all of this,' said Big Hard Face, 'and in return you wish no horses?'

'I have made the bargain,' said Walking Horse, 'and I have received your word under witness of Tarawa. You will accept in turn what I am to give you and keep it in your teepee. You and Thunder Moon . . . you will guard it carefully?'

'That is all agreed,' said Big Hard Face impatiently. 'Now, brother, what is this thing?'

Walking Horse turned sharply around and made an imperious gesture. The girl at once dismounted and, taking her hand, Walking Horse placed it in the hand of Thunder Moon.

'Other men,' he said, 'accept great gifts for a daughter, and especially for a beautiful girl. Instead, I offer the price of fifty horses to the man who will accept her. Her name is Red Wind. Take her as you have sworn to do. Put her in your lodge. Guard her well and keep her. Make her your squaw if you will. But watch her always.'

Thunder Moon was stunned. He looked down to the soft, slender hand which lay in his. He looked up to the face of the girl and saw that her eyes were not black, but the deepest, darkest shade of blue, like the color of water at dusk – almost like the color of the midnight sky.

They passed into the teepee. Big Hard Face, his doubts ended, began to laugh a little, and his old eyes shone as he looked to Walking Horse.

'Brother,' he said, 'you have given us two gifts, and the first was worth fifty fine horses, but the second looks to me still more valuable.'

Walking Horse, in place of replying, smiled most sourly. Then he turned on the girl. 'I have brought you into a new life,' he said to her in a stern voice. 'Among the Omissis, you have made much trouble. Twenty men have had their knives ready for my throat because of you. There has been no peace among us for five years. Now I take you to another tribe. Guard your voice. Take heed when you sing. Keep your head covered. Learn cookery and the dressing of skins. It may be that you will become a blessing to Thunder Moon. But make such trouble in his lodge as you have made in mine and be sure that he will take you with one hand and crush out your life as a boy catches a small bird and crushes it to death. I have spoken.'

With this bitter farewell, he turned upon his heel and left the teepee. Big Hard Face overtook him just outside.

'Walking Horse,' he said, 'we are friends. When two friends are together, they point out to one another the dangers that threaten him. Now, you see a danger. You see that there is a storm ahead, but Thunder Moon and I cannot see it. Tell us then, from what direction it may blow.'

'I shall tell you,' said Walking Horse, half sternly and half in sorrow. 'From this moment, there is danger all around you. It lies down by your side at night; it walks beside you in the dusk. It slides in the shadow of your galloping horse, and it hangs in the sky above you. Danger blows toward you from every corner of the sky.'

Big Hard Face became sober indeed. 'Brother,' he entreated, 'we look and we see only a beautiful girl. The color of her hair is strange. But it is not unpleasant. Otherwise, she seems what a woman should be. Tell us, therefore, in what way she may harm us?'

'You are not a young man,' said the Omissis, unrelenting. 'I am not a boy and yet you could be my father. You are the chief who leads a great tribe, and the councils of Big Hard Face have made the Suhtai rich and great on the plains. You have a great warrior in your lodge. There is no other like him among all the Cheyennes. Between you, you may discover the danger for yourselves. It may be that no danger at all will be seen. The Sky People listen to the voice of Thunder Moon. They may teach him what to do and how to make a wild bird sing songs. I have been long from my people and they need me. We have been in great trouble. I have lived for five years with the knife at my throat. Now I shall go back to my lodge and lie down to a long sleep. Farewell. Be wise. Let White Crow keep her eyes open every day and every night.'

With this he turned away and mounted his horse and was gone, followed instantly by the Omissis who had driven in the pack train.

# 12

# Evil Spirits

The pursuit of the five lost horses was forgotten. Thunder Moon went back into the lodge and found the maiden standing with her hands folded together as close to the wall of the teepee as she could get. The prisoner, Rising Cloud, turned the eyes which had been watching her toward his captor, and it seemed to the latter that there was a touch of keen envy in the expression of the Pawnee.

'You have ridden on a long trail,' said Thunder Moon to the girl. 'Sit down. White Crow, put meat before her.'

'This is fitting?' said the old hag, her withered face growing black with anger. 'I must wait on a slave who has been given away by her own father because of the evil that is in her. I must wait on her. I shall not lift my hand to help her.'

'It is true that I must serve myself,' said the girl meekly, and would have then, but Thunder Moon with a gesture made her sit down again.

'What evil is there in her?' he asked his foster aunt.

The hag went to the girl with long strides and laid hold on a heavy coil of the copper-red hair. 'There is danger in this, worse than fire,' she said.

'Fire?' murmured Thunder Moon, astonished. He knew nothing of women. They had not crossed so much as the very threshold of his life.

'You will soon be in flames,' said White Crow, sneering again.

'There is danger in this also,' she went on and, placing her bony hand under the soft chin of Red Wind, she forced up her face and pointed to the great blue eyes and to the lips, parted as though in fear.

'What danger?' asked Thunder Moon.

'You have lived all these years in my teepee,' said White Crow, 'and still you are a fool.' In the meantime, she placed a dish of meat before Red Wind, and then hurried from the teepee, as though fearing that she might be called upon for other services.

Thunder Moon reached forth his mighty hand and took up a braid of the hair gingerly. 'I see no danger in this,' he said simply. 'And in no other Cheyenne maiden or man have I looked into blue eyes. But is there a wrong in the color? You, Rising Cloud, are a wise man and a chief, and the brother of a chief. Tell me if there is danger?'

The wind had been rising and now it increased heavily. The patch of sun which fell through the opened flap of the teepee was darkened suddenly as though the sky had been overcast. Rising Cloud, before he answered, raised his head and seemed to listen to the storm. Then he looked at Thunder Moon.

'Oh, my brother,' he said, 'sometimes the trail cannot be followed by the sign, and sometimes the mind travels where words cannot go.'

Very often an Indian expresses himself in some such obscure fashion, letting his meaning be hinted at rather than spoken and defined. Most of the Cheyennes were experts in deciphering such hidden meanings, but the foster son of Big Hard Face ever was dull at this exercise of the wits. He shook his head and looked back to the girl.

'Tell me,' he said, 'in what manner Walking Horse has found evil and trouble in you?'

She looked down and sighed meekly. 'My father never has loved me,' she said. 'Who can tell why? Evil spirits surely stand between him and me.'

It seemed to Thunder Moon that from the corner of his eye he saw his prisoner smiling, but he could not be sure.

'Eat!' he said.

'I am not hungry,' she said.

'Have you had food today?'

'No.'

'Then you are hungry.'

She lifted her large eyes to him. They were filled with tears. 'Fear and hunger are not brothers, oh, Thunder Moon,' she said.

'Are you afraid?'

'I have been brought like a dog and flung into the lodge of a man who does not want me,' she said. 'I am among strange people and my heart turns to water.'

The soul of Thunder Moon swelled within him. He flashed a glance over his shoulder as though daring danger to approach. Then he said: 'I have not said that you are not welcome here. You are very welcome. No danger shall come near you. As for White Crow, she is so old that she is losing her wits. Now eat. I myself, Thunder Moon, tell you not to be afraid.'

She began obediently to eat with such a wonderful daintiness as he never had seen before. Every time she raised her fingers to her lips, her eyes went up child-like, resting for a moment upon the stern face of her new master, as though asking for further permission.

Thunder Moon began to smile a little, and nodded continually. He was on the verge of pointing out choice morsels, as a squaw does for her child. It seemed to him that Rising Cloud also was smiling continually, faintly, though whenever Thunder Moon looked fairly at him the Pawnee's face was grave enough. Something was wrong, he felt. What it could be he was unable to guess and before long he discovered that he did not care.

'Thunder Moon is happy,' said the Pawnee suddenly.

'Yes,' said the warrior, but corrected himself to add: 'Sad, also, my friend.'

'Your teepee is filled with treasure. A beautiful woman has been given to you. Why should you be sad, Thunder Moon?'

The maiden ceased eating so that she might listen.

'I am sad, Rising Cloud, when I think that such a girl, young, beautiful and good, could be hated by her own father. That is what makes my heart heavy.'

The maiden continued her meal.

Shouting and confusion began to come upon the village. The wind had increased to hurricane dimensions. Clouds of dust began to invade the teepee of Big Hard Face, sifting through imperceptible crevices. Now and again a lodge went down with a crash before the cuffing of the storm.

Thunder Moon went to the flap of the lodge and watched the vast masses of the storm mist hurtling across the whole face of the heavens. He saw the frightened Indians working furiously to make fast their lodges while some unlucky families, screaming for the help of their neighbors, struggled away to secure their possessions after the lodge had been blown from above their heads.

Big Hard Face came hastily into the teepee, pressing past his foster son unceremoniously. 'The Wind Spirits are angered, child,' he said, as he passed. 'I shall make medicine. Come and help me. Where is White Crow?'

Big Hard Face was as hard-headed as any man in the tribe but, like all the rest, these disturbances of the sky troubled him. They were the direct manifestations of the power of an angered deity. To Thunder Moon, however, they had a different significance. Since that day in his youth when he had first conceived that the Sky People had taken him under their particular protection, all the phenomena of the air fascinated him. If there were danger, and if these prodigious outbursts showed the limitless strength of the spirits, nevertheless it seemed to him like the wrath shown by a friend and therefore a passion which would be sure to leave him unscathed.

The doorway of the teepee was to him bethel. From that place he had stared at the sky many an hour and, watching its changing lights and drifting clouds, he had felt as though he were looking into the mind of Tarawa. This thronging legion of the storm spirits seemed to him an army singing a canticle in praise of the Sky People and he wanted to raise his voice to add to the tumult. He controlled himself, however, for he knew that it would have seemed to the rest of his people a mysterious sort of blasphemy.

He saw Spotted Bull, dressed in the hideous costume of his profession, staggering against the wind and approaching as rapidly as he could, followed by half a dozen of the chief men of the Suhtai. When he came nearer, Spotted Bull turned slowly into the lodge of Big Hard Face, crying: 'Make way, Thunder Moon! This storm is of your raising. You have brought evil into this camp and, unless I drive it out, the Sky People will tear up all our lodges and then tear up the Suhtai also, and send us whirling away through the air forever.'

Saying this, he pressed past the warrior and entered the lodge with his companions at his heels and, the instant he was inside, he stretched out his arm toward Red Wind.

'It is in her!' cried Spotted Bull. 'The evil is in her, and Thunder Moon has brought her into his lodge.'

'Drive her out!' shouted Gray Eagle, one of those with Spotted

Bull. 'Drive her out at once from the town. My lodge is staggering. Soon it will go down. The teepees of Snake-That-Talks and Two White Feathers have been snatched away into the air. Drive her out at once.'

White Crow caught the girl by the arm and tugged at her. 'Get up, witch!' she shrieked. 'Get up and go.'

Thunder Moon strode suddenly between his foster aunt and the girl. 'You are all fools,' he said. 'I have shown you once within a day that Spotted Bull is a fool and a coward. The Sky People are angry. But not at us. Only they are shaking our town a little as they rush away toward the mountains.'

Spotted Bull, his face dark with malignity, stared at the youth and quivered with rage, but presently he shouted: 'I will show you what my power is, Thunder Moon. I will show you that I could wither you up like a leaf, if I chose. I pity you. I shall not drive this woman away. I shall purify her, and presently the Sky People will make the day clean again above our heads.'

Thunder crashed at that instant and such a terrible lightning bolt leaped down from the sky that through the seams and the cracks of the tent it cast a bright flicker of light on those inside. With a groan, they cowered toward the earth – all save Thunder Moon and the girl who kept her eyes fixed upon his face, as though half bewitched by his calm courage.

'Make haste, Spotted Bull!' cried Big Hard Face. 'Make haste. I feel the Sky People pluck at the top of my lodge. The earth trembles. In another moment all of us will be whirled away.'

# 13

# Dear Danger

Thunder Moon, at this entreaty, relented in so much that he stood back a little, merely saying to the girl: 'Do not be afraid. Spotted Bull dares not harm you. He is a fool. I have proved it before. He will prove it himself by trying to stop this storm. That will be the end of him.'

So said the warrior sneering at the medicine man. The latter, in fact, understood his position perfectly well. The disastrous inaccuracy of his late prophecies which had been meant to depress the influence of Thunder Moon had, instead, reared the fame of the young brave like a temple built of massive ashlar. For lesser failures than these, medicine men had been put to death as though they were dogs. Had not Thunder Moon possessed singular gentleness of spirit for a Cheyenne, the fatal blow certainly would have fallen upon the false doctor when the hero returned to camp with his prisoner. Even as it was, Spotted Bull was in a perilous position. His power had melted away. He stood upon dissolving sands. Accordingly, he had seized upon the opportunity which the storm gave him of proclaiming the vengeance of the spirits upon Thunder Moon.

No matter how much the chiefs might doubt the power of Spotted Bull's medicine, they were too frightened not to listen to him with attention and watch for possible results. By the springing of a sudden trap, the medicine man found himself committed to the desperate task of banishing the storm itself from the sky.

He fell to work with a perfect fury, dancing wildly around the Omissis girl, who stood with her hands clasped and her head bowed, staring at the ground in quiet submission. Perhaps the passion of Spotted Bull was bipartite, partly assumed in a frenzy of fear, and in one portion really composed of a mysterious confidence that he was in touch with the spirits of the upper air.

The necklace of bear claws leaped and rattled upon his neck. Sweat streamed down his face and body. His headdress waved and nodded madly. All the time he kept up a prodigious racket by beating a rattle which he held in one hand against a drum which he held in the other. In the meantime, he shouted forth in a chant confused words of Delphic import and only paused once or twice to throw a handful of sweet grass upon the fire, the smoke of which rose with the prevailing current of the air and covered the form of Red Wind with fragrant mist.

Through that mist Spotted Bull was seen still leaping and gesticulating, until finally he paused and struck an imposing attitude before the maiden and shouted: 'Spirits of storm and terror, I see you. I have forced you to come down. Like a white eagle your king sits on the head of this girl. I see you. I name you. I command you to be gone. Be gone! Be gone!'

The only answer to Spotted Bull was a vast peal of thunder and then again a perfect torrent of lightning flooding down from the sky, followed by deadening volleys as though all the powers of the universe had joined in a sort of mammoth derrydown to maintain the burden of this terrible song of wrath.

'See?' laughed Thunder Moon. 'He is ten times a fool!'

The others could not see, however. Fear crushed their bodies and their hearts against the ground. Only the medicine man, Thunder Moon, and the girl remained erect, while Big Hard Face called hopelessly: 'Kill Spotted Bull. He only angers the spirits. He will have us all destroyed.'

Spotted Bull apparently saw death literally rubbing elbows with him and he bellowed out: 'Yell and shout, evil winds! Pour down your fires! You are angry, because I am your master. The Sky People will hear me. They will herd you out of the sky like buffalo before the hunters. Go! Go! Go!'

So shouted the medicine man, and the prostrate, frightened Suhtai closed their ears and shut their eyes, expecting another roar of heavenly artillery. Presently it came, but at an amazing distance. With a sudden inspiration, Spotted Bull rushed to the flap of the lodge and tore it open. There he stood, pointing above him with an arm stiffened by excitement and shrieked.

'Now, come to see! I have been heard. The storm runs away. Be gone, black clouds! I command you! Fall down the slope of the sky! Let the sun shine upon us! Give us your brightness and your heat! Let your rays tell the Suhtai that Spotted Bull has good medicine . . . has great medicine . . . that he can command even the winds, and he holds the lightnings even in his bare hands.'

So screamed Spotted Bull, and the people in the tent hurried to the open flap and stared up to the sky; and there they saw – most miraculous! – that the deep masses of the clouds had parted and rolled away to either side, and now, even as the medicine man spoke, the shadows were parted from before the face of the sun and all the golden tide of his brilliance streamed once again over the earth. At that, as the wind fell suddenly away, a great song of rejoicing rose from the entire village, but it was as nothing compared with the excitement in the teepee of Big Hard Face. He himself, though he was a thrifty soul, picked up a fine new rifle and thrust it into the hands of the great medicine man. All the others followed suit by presenting gifts of some sort or promising others when they could get them.

By this lucky stroke, Spotted Bull had swept into the forgotten past the little matter of his false prophecy concerning Thunder Moon and the war trail. Nothing succeeds like success, particularly like the success of today as against whatever may have happened yesterday. He was more than a luminary. He was literally a great binary that filled the whole eye of the Cheyennes at that moment for partly he was a hero for having defied the evil spirits of the storm and dared their wrath in person, partly he was a divine medicine man. His own joy was as tremendous as his fear and his despair had been great only a few moments before.

Literally staggering, so dizzy was his head with his glory, he turned on Big Hard Face and said: 'The maiden is purified. Now she cannot harm our tribe. As for the young man' – and here he pointed carelessly toward the famous Thunder Moon – 'you have seen that I could have poured a river of lightning upon him if I chose. But I am merciful. I remember that he is young and that he lives in the teepee of a good friend, Big Hard Face. So I am merciful.'

He left, surrounded by the chiefs. Big Hard Face hurried after him to join the chorus of praise.

There remained in the lodge the Pawnee, just recovering from sheer terror, Thunder Moon, and the girl. She had not stirred from her graceful position and Thunder Moon, staring at her, half thought that he saw the drifting smoke of the sweet grass form above her head in the dim outline of an eagle. He thrust the superstitious fancy from his mind.

'Is it ended?' asked the girl.

He nodded.

'And may I move?'

'You may. You are free to go where you will, Red Wind. The young men will show you my horses. Of all that is in this teepee you may make your choice. Of the rifles and the ammunition. Do as you will with them. I shall not force you to remain here.'

'Ah,' said the girl, 'do you drive me out, also?'

'I?' cried Thunder Moon. 'No, but you ask me if you are free to move and I tell you that you are as free as the lightning in the sky. Go where you will.'

'Where could I go? I am homeless in the world,' she said, and sighed deeply.

'You forget, Thunder Moon,' broke in the dry voice of the young Pawnee, 'you have given your word to keep this maiden.'

Thunder Moon, recovering from his enthusiasm, bit his lip and darted an angry glance at the prisoner. The latter was looking intently at the girl and apparently did not notice the wrath of his captor. She, however, had lifted her head and looked with mild eyes on the shining treasure of the guns.

'In the middle of the storm,' said Thunder Moon suddenly, 'you were not frightened, Red Wind. While the rest . . . and even Rising Cloud, yonder . . . shrank and trembled, you were not afraid.'

Her large, gentle eyes turned to him and dwelt upon him and his heart began to flutter with something like fear, though delight was blended mysteriously with it.

'You stood near me,' said Red Wind. 'I knew that you would protect me. The Sky People are like brothers to Thunder Moon. They never would step into his lodge.'

This speech made Thunder Moon fairly giddy and he went slowly to the entrance to the lodge, and paused there. His heart was beating at a prodigious rate. What he was to do he had not the slightest idea, but he felt that something was expected from him. Or, rather, it was as though a vast opportunity had opened before him, and how to use it was not given him to understand. He did know that the Pawnee was smiling again, knew it, though his back was turned to the captive.

Outside the village was in an uproar. He could see a shouting crowd gather around the proud form of Spotted Bull who was making a speech, in which he doubtless had much to say about his familiarity with the spirits and in which he congratulated the Suhtai on having such a person as himself among them. Thunder Moon smiled a little in turn, a grim smile, and then he looked back to the girl.

She no longer seemed an Omissis maiden in the teepee of Big Hard Face, chief of the Suhtai. The last smoke of the sweet grass clung to the ground about her feet, and a wisp of it shrouded her faintly, and the red-gold of her hair shone through. To Thunder Moon she was of more than an earthly beauty. It was as though he stood in the very presence of a dream that was not a dream. She was to him like some strange vision of Ashtoreth standing in a field of white flowered asphodel, smiling, and with profound mystery in her smile.

He wanted to speak. Words would not come. He was dizzier than before. He stepped out into the open air and looked up to the blue of the sky from which the storm had been brushed away so oddly. He had no faith in the astral pretensions of the medicine man but, in spite of himself, he could not help feeling that there was danger indeed in the presence of the Omissis girl.

# 14

# Brothers

Big Hard Face was a man of practical mind and he quickly recovered from the shocks of that day's events – the presentation of the treasure, the coming of the girl, the mystery of the storm, and the big medicine which had banished it. He reverted to the subject of the stolen horses and went to his foster son to urge him out on the trail. He found Thunder Moon like one in a trance, looking up to the sky which had given him inspiration so often but which failed him now, utterly.

'Then I ride myself!' said the old man hotly. 'You have been bewitched and turned into a deaf stone and you are no longer a man, Thunder Moon.'

He would, in fact, have departed at once with a chosen band of braves had it not been for the arrival of a messenger who raced his pony through the village and flung himself down in front of Big Hard Face, gasping out a strange message.

He had ridden out onto the prairie after the storm to help locate the horses which might have been driven astray by the fury of the wind and, venturing far out, suddenly a Pawnee riding a tall chestnut horse barred his return to the village and covered him with a rifle. Boy though he was, and armed only with a knife, he would have fought for life and scalp. The Pawnee offered him peace and good will and merely bade him go into the village and carry word to Big Hard Face and particularly to Thunder Moon that the Pawnees were ready to bury the hatchet and welcome peace, if Thunder Moon would set free Rising Cloud. In return, the Pawnees would return all the ponies they had captured during the raid. Particularly, as an earnest of good faith, they engaged to send in immediately, upon an appointed signal, the five chestnuts which had been stolen the day before. The Pawnees would give up the chestnuts merely as a signal of their desire for peace, but first they must be assured that their messenger would receive no harm at the hands of the Suhtai.

To such a proposal as this there could be only one answer. The appointed smoke signal was sent up at once. The wailing of the squaws which was rising from all quarters of the camp in dreary assonance ceased and the curious mob began to assemble to see the Pawnee come in.

What a roar rose from the outskirts of the town when the Pawnee came. It swept closer. Big Hard Face was discovered in close and eager conference with his son. He was entreating Thunder Moon to listen to reason and agree to deliver up the captured Pawnee. For there was only a definite value to be attached to all things – even to such a splendid exploit as that of Thunder Moon in the Pawnee camp. But the foster son of the chief was gloomily silent. Only his eyes flashed when, through the opening gap in the crowd of the Suhtai, he saw a warrior with the cropped head of a Pawnee mounted on a spirited pinto and leading behind him the five beautiful chestnuts which had been stolen from his father's herd.

Coming up to the lodge of Big Hard Face, in front of which that chieftain stood, the newcomer dismounted and saluted the Suhtai with much dignity, regardless of the savage hatred of the squaws. They were pushing forward eagerly, anxious to have clearer sight of this man who had had some hand, doubtless, in the slaying of the lost Suhtai. Before the messenger could speak, a young warrior cried out in a thrilling voice: 'Beware! It is Falling Stone himself. It is the new war chief of the Pawnees.'

That startling suggestion reduced even the squaws to silence. All, in a hushed reverence that was almost fear, pressed closer to stare at the victorious leader who had struck them such a dreadful blow. There was little about him to suggest that he might be the brother of the handsome and graceful brave, Rising Cloud. Low-browed, with wide cheekbones and heavy, brutal jaw, he looked like the lowest type of plains Indian. His eyes, though, were bright and clear. When he spoke, one felt instantly the presence of a reasoning and keen intelligence.

Moreover, though his body was scarcely more beautiful than his face, it was framed on such massive lines of strength that even Thunder Moon scanned the figure of the leader with something like apprehension. All the striking and gripping muscles along his arms and in his mighty hands grew taut, as though he were stepping into combat with that chieftain at once.

Falling Stone said simply: 'The son of my father and my mother is in the teepee of Thunder Moon. The lodge and the heart of my father are empty. I have come to ask for Rising Cloud. Give him to me, oh, Suhtai, and take in exchange my friendship and these horses as a pledge of it.'

'My friend,' answered Big Hard Face, looking intently at the other, 'you have taken away many of my young men and you have brought us much sorrow. Every man must do his own work, and the work of a Pawnee and a Suhtai cannot be the same. I am willing to talk to you about setting your brother free. You offer five horses. It is very well. But that is not the price of your brother, I believe.'

'I offer all the ponies which you lost when I was last in this camp,' replied the Pawnee.

'And how many is that, Falling Stone?'

'You, yourself, can count them, my father.'

'We have counted our losses. Three hundred and fifty horses which were grazed by our young men have been lost.'

'They are not all in my hands,' replied the other. 'Yet I can give more than three hundred.'

'It is not in my heart to make a close bargain,' said Big Hard Face, with pretended generosity. 'Let it all be as you choose. Send me the three hundred ponies and you shall have your brother. . . .'

'If it is my will,' broke in Thunder Moon sternly.

'In the camp of the Pawnees,' replied Falling Stone, with cunning rebuke implied, 'when one speaks to the father, one is also speaking to the son.'

'True, true!' said Big Hard Face, speaking hastily and apparently out of the ebullient good nature which was in him. 'Let it be as. . . .'

'Father,' said Thunder Moon, 'I must be heard. Let us go into the lodge. The children and the women listen to us. It is better to speak to a few than to many.'

'It is true,' said Big Hard Face. 'There are no brains in a crowd. It has no head.' He ushered them into his lodge with much dignity.

The Pawnee brothers stood face to face again and it was curious to watch their behavior. Undoubtedly in their own home they would have rushed into one another's arms, but here they were before strangers and they gave one another only a glance and a quiet word. The contrast between them was sharper than before. The war chief looked more abysmally brutish; the prisoner seemed more wonderfully graceful and capable of swift movement. One was a mastiff, the other a greyhound.

'Here in a Suhtai lodge, and living, I never expected to find you,' said Falling Stone.

His brother answered in a soft and rapid voice: 'I woke up with the knife of that man at my throat. He asked if I were the leader of the war party. Should I have said no, brother?'

Falling Stone cast a sharp glance of inquiry at Thunder Moon, who replied with equal brevity. 'He gave himself to me in your place. I looked at both of you. When your eyes were closed in sleep, I could not guess that you were the leader.'

Falling Stone cast one eloquent glance of affection toward his brother and then was silent, waiting with courtly majesty and composure.

Thunder Moon said abruptly: 'You have brought back to us five horses as a pledge of good faith. I shall buy back those horses. There are rifles in that heap, as you may see for yourself. They are not common horses. I offer no common price. Take five rifles for each.'

The eyes of the war chief glistened, and Big Hard Face broke in: 'Boy, you put lightning in the hands of one who will pour it on your own head!'

'I have made the offer,' said Thunder Moon, frowning at the interruption.

'It is taken!' said the chief. 'The horses are yours again. These are mine.' He could not avoid picking up one of the rifles and he put it down with the lingering touch of one who loved the weapons. Perhaps already he was imagining a score of his best followers mounted on good horses and equipped with these new and first-rate guns. The picture filled his mind's eye, for he was no carpet knight, but a hero who had advanced by battle alone.

'I take the rifles,' he said, 'and give back the horses. I accept the price which you offer. Does that deprive me of the right to buy back the freedom of my brother?'

'No,' said Big Hard Face eagerly. 'The fifty horses. . . .'

'Father,' interrupted Thunder Moon, 'I have offered a great price and bought back your horses. Now I talk of a thing which is purely mine . . . not mine, but belonging to the Sky People. That is Rising Cloud. The white spirit of the moon and the Sky People led me into the Pawnee camp. They made my feet silent even in the dead grass. They used my hand to kill three men. They gave me a chief as a captive. They carried me out of the camp again. They sheltered me when I escaped, putting a mist over the eyes of my enemies. I offered them a sacrifice. A great sacrifice. Now I swear it. Rising Cloud must die to do them honor!'

The prisoner was silent, but a deep groan was wrung from the throat of his brother. There was a slight flash of light and Thunder Moon saw that it was the Omissis girl, turning gravely toward the captive. In this light her hair was like the red of carnelian, shot with gold. Her eyes said nothing and her face was like a mask.

'We two shall meet!' cried Falling Stone in a fury of grief and of hate. Big Hard Face, thinking of the fifty lost horses, covered his head and withdrew from the conference – a mute recognition that his authority over his foster son had reached a sharply defined limit.

'Let us meet, then,' answered Thunder Moon instantly. 'Let us take out your brother, still bound, into the prairie beyond the village. There you and I shall fight for him. He who wins takes him.'

'Is it agreed?' asked the Pawnee eagerly.

'No,' broke in Rising Cloud. 'Listen to me, my brother. You are great in war. This man fights with a strange medicine. The spirits point his guns. With that one which has six bullets, he knocks down the rabbits as they run. If you fight with him, you die! I have seen him. I understand.'

Falling Stone, writhing with shame and with envious grief, cried out: 'And you, brother?'

'As for me,' said Rising Cloud, with the calm of a true eclectic who has considered many forms of life and thought and found them all light things, 'as for me, I die with no dishonor and shall be buried without shame. Thunder Moon has given me that promise. You . . . go back to our people. You cannot struggle against the medicine of this pale-faced Cheyenne. Do not forget me. When you lead out your war bands, let the braves shout my name when they charge. Many Suhtai shall die for my sake.'

It was no mere blazon of indifference which the captive showed, but a true resignation, and his brother looked long and earnestly upon him.

'No man will believe that I have refused to fight for your sake, Rising Cloud,' he said. 'I am a naked warrior and Thunder Moon is shielded by the spirits. Only the Sky People could have led him into our camp through all the warriors. Do you forgive me if I ride away?'

'I forgive you with all my heart,' said the prisoner. 'Farewell!'

Falling Stone went slowly from the teepee. As he passed out, Thunder Moon stepped softly after him. 'I shall leave my guns behind me,' he said. 'Let us ride out with shield and spear and knife only, my friend. If you go back to your people with your brother and with the scalp of Thunder Moon, you will be the greatest hero who ever rode into the city of the Pawnees.'

Falling Stone regarded him with an odd mixture of hate and fear and wonder.

'Is it only a bullet that a spirit can guide straight?' he said. 'I live and fight by the strength of my hand. I leave medicine to the medicine makers. Say no more, for I shall not fight with you unless I see you in the middle of battle. Then be sure that I shall not go backward.'

The guns were loaded upon the pony which he rode and Falling Stone departed slowly from the camp, riding with bowed head. Had Thunder Moon been a true Indian, he could not have helped pushing his advantage and, to shame the Pawnee, ride after him and taunt him loudly on his way through the camp. But he was not a true Indian. As a matter of fact, he felt a certain degree of sympathy with Falling Stone for Thunder Moon himself believed that his great deeds in war were produced more by a singular diablerie with which the Sky People had endowed him than by his native strength of hand and of spirit. His heart began to rise. Now that the five lost steeds had been returned and paid for out of the price of the maiden, it seemed that a crown of good fortune had been placed upon the head of Thunder Moon. Only one thing remained for him to do, and that was to return to the Sky People the reward which he had promised them. Many sacrifices he had offered before, but never a human life.

He went back into his lodge. 'The time has come, Rising Cloud,' he said. 'Stand up and come with me.'

# 15

# And Yet a Woman

If in many ways Thunder Moon fell short of the wild cruelty of which an Indian was capable, yet it is equally true that no Indian ever could have sacrificed a human life with the calm of spirit which now possessed the warrior. To him it was a spiritual rather than a physical act and, by many dexter signs, he was convinced of the kindness of the spirit world and felt that he must make this great return to the Sky People.

The Pawnee, without a word, stood up and prepared to go with him. They had crossed halfway through the teepee when the soft, gentle voice of the Omissis girl said: 'Oh, Thunder Moon, why do you sacrifice now when the Sky People are far up in the heavens, living in the light of the sun where it is brightest and hottest? Do not give this man to the moon spirit or the sky, but wait until the dawn of tomorrow has filled the sky with rosy light, for then the Sky People are so close that we can hear the whispering of their feathers as they pass by.'

There is an ecumenical rule that he who proceeds calmly to action by calmness may be dissuaded. So it was now. The passionate man is the hasty man, but there was no passion in Thunder Moon now. He hesitated and then he smiled at the girl.

'How much truth there is in you!' he said. 'How much wisdom. Yet you are a woman and you are not old. When I look at you, Red

Wind, I feel that I am rich. There is no man among the Cheyennes who is so rich as I am in having you.'

So saying, he gave up his purpose of the immediate sacrifice and went hastily out from the tent. After the storm all the prairie was fresh. The ground was soft. The horses would be running wildly and gaily. The children would be dancing and singing and tumbling one over another. There was something in the heart of the warrior which sympathized with all this physical activity and made him a part of all that he looked upon. He passed White Crow crouching by the lodge entrance. She stopped him with one of her keen, cruel glances that probed a man to the soul.

'She is yours, but she is not really yours. You have not married her, Thunder Moon.'

He stopped, frowning.

'What keeps you back?' asked the crone in her snarling voice.

Thunder Moon began to think aloud, purposely looking away from the ugly face of the old squaw. 'Now that she is in the lodge, she is mine to look at and listen to. If I ask her to marry me. . . .'

'You do not have to ask. She is yours to be taken!'

'I never could do that. For all I know, she may have a lover among the Omissis.'

'Would you give her up, my dear son, if she begged you to set her free and let her go to another man?'

Still Thunder Moon was silent. His forehead glistened. With the edged tool of her tongue she had wounded him again.

'But if I ask her to marry me,' went on Thunder Moon, boggling his words rather badly, 'perhaps she will say that she does not wish to live in my lodge. Then what? Could I keep her? She would scorn me. I could not endure that. No. It is better to keep her as she is. For a while.'

The hag began to laugh, showing her pale, withered gums in the ecstasy of her mirth. 'I shall tell you what really is in your mind.'

'Tell me, then,' he asked, diligently avoiding her with his eyes.

A boy playing with the cascabel of a rattlesnake went by them, and the eyes of the crone followed him for a moment before she spoke again. 'I shall tell you, Thunder Moon. The spirits speak to you, do they not? They guide you?'

'Sometimes they do when I pray to them.'

'And sometimes when you do not pray. What spirits did you know to pray to when you were first a boy in this camp? Still, you lived. Well, the spirits speak in you. Those spirits now say to you: "Leave that woman alone! Do not go near her. She is dangerous." '

'How could she be dangerous to me, White Crow?'

'You do not fear her because she has given you no warning. But I tell you a thing. A rattlesnake makes a noise before it strikes. A woman makes no noise. She smiles before she stabs you.'

He drew himself up in a sort of diaconal stiffness and dignity, saying: 'You are too old to remember the mind of a pure girl. Do not talk to me any more about her. Mind your pots of meat and make the buffalo robes and keep your thoughts away from important matters.'

Thus spoke Thunder Moon, terrible in his surety and in his pride. The old hag simply answered: 'Does she make you happy?'

Her foster nephew said nothing.

'Well,' she said, 'let me tell you that one day she will bring you much more grief than all of the sorrow that is in the hearts of those wailing squaws!'

For the mourners had withdrawn from the camp. By the river or on hummocks of ground nearby on the prairie, they were raising their laments, tearing open their wounds, beating their heads, writhing in the dust, and their voices came out of the distance mingled and softened but deep with meaning. The gates of the heart of Thunder Moon were opened, and he felt that he was hearing the diapason of life, its fundamental harmony of sorrow and of despair.

'Never has a wolf made a kill,' said Thunder Moon in a sudden passion of anger, 'without the envious howl of a coyote close at hand. So it is with you. You have forgotten happiness. You would like to send it all out of the world.'

He walked hastily away, deep in a mist of thought. Yet he could not go unnoticed. Whenever he stirred forth, a band of the striplings was sure to gather instantly around him for, at times, he was known to give much attention to them, telling them odd stories of his hunting and his fighting, talking more easily with them than with the men of the tribe.

They gathered about him, hopefully watching his face, and then trailing behind. Perhaps – who could tell? – he even would let them handle his knife which had drunk the blood of so many enemies or even fire his revolver. For he had done it before. And then he was possessed of an infinite store of wisdom such as boys prize. Whatever he could do, he could describe and therefore he could teach. Accordingly, as a teacher of wrestling and boxing and running and leaping and swimming, he was matchless.

A little legion attended him whenever he walked abroad, running ahead, pulling from his path a dog or a little child that happened to be in his way, and even shouting to the women and to the warriors: 'Step out of the way there, and be quick about it! Thunder Moon is coming.'

The women, of course, scattered willingly and quickly enough. One and all, they were in deadly terror of a medicine man and Thunder Moon was surrounded in part by the dignity of a warrior and in part by the efferent mystery which was breathed out around a medicine man and worker in wizardry. The warriors moved more slowly from his way, grudging his greatness, but afraid of him also.

He went through the little village like a sort of superior being. Certainly by his passing he did not edify the morals of his compeers, but left behind him a trail of envy and wrath and subdued but fierce malice. So it is always with the great ones of the world. The danger of Thunder Moon was all the more poignant because in his absent-minded course of living he never dreamed what wild jealousies sprang up around him. Who was there to tell him of the truth? No one, perhaps, except White Crow and, by the continual gloom of her forebodings, she had caused herself to be disregarded in her teepee almost as completely as another Cassandra.

Down to the river went Thunder Moon and sat on a stump and regarded the darkly swirling waters. He picked up a stone and idly he cast it into the stream. Instantly half a dozen flashing bodies leaped from the band and dived into the water. The victor emerged with the stone in his hand and laid it with a smile of pleasure at the feet of Thunder Moon. He stepped back and waited for a word of commendation – a glistening, slender young statue of red copper.

At length, the warrior looked up. Like a dancer in the bolero, so his brain was reeling and swaying with emotion which was new to him. He looked up and saw the children. He saw the dripping boy. He saw the wet stone at his feet. Suddenly Thunder Moon sighed. Some day he would like to have sons like these, slender, swift footed, bright eyed. He suddenly sprang to his feet. He would marry Red Wind, come of it what might!

He started back toward the village and, as he went, the unending wails of the mourners sang a dreary monody in his ears.

# 16

# The Price of Manhood

His little legion followed him. They were used to his absent-minded ways and therefore they did not show their disappointment. They escorted him through the village as they had escorted him out of it, worshipping him with their eyes, clearing the way before him, and dispersing at last when he came to his lodge.

Thunder Moon went straight in and found Red Wind braiding her hair, while White Crow snarled softly to herself in a corner of the teepee, sewing beads upon a pair of moccasins. The captive as ever sat erect, at ease, his eyes a blank.

'Red Wind,' said Thunder Moon, 'I have come to say a solemn thing to you.'

She looked up to him and saw in his face such pure emotion as might have served for song by the verge of old Castalia, and her fingers froze in the solid, metal masses of her braids.

'Master,' she said, 'I hear you.'

'I have given my oath to keep you in my lodge. Let me keep you as my wife.'

Her great blue eyes dwelt upon him as though in fear. Slowly her fingers resumed the thoughtless work of braiding her hair.

'Of all the Cheyennes you are the greatest and the richest,' she said. 'I am only your slave. It is pity that makes you speak to me like this. Wait until the morning when you offer a life to the Sky People.

Ask them then if you should do this thing. Then your will must be my will.'

She had not repelled him, and yet he felt the repulsion. Out of the distance he heard again the drifting, melancholy music of the mourning women. From the side of the teepee he saw the evil grin of White Crow as she bent over her work. Then it occurred to him suddenly, that no other Cheyenne would have spoken of such a thing to a maiden before listeners. He was shamed and, in his shame, he withdrew from the girl. Like a shadow of prophetic spirit he saw dimly before him a shaping and forecasting of trouble. Gradually, therefore, it seemed to him more and more clear that he should have approached her in a different manner, but still he was reasonably certain that all would eventually go well. When he looked at himself as at a picture, he could not help seeing that he was all that the girl had said. The greatest and the richest man among the Cheyennes.

The thought comforted him. That night, as he sat on his couch and smoked before sleeping, he watched the others go to bed one by one, dropping the end curtain of soft antelope skins which shut off each compartment from the sight of the central portion of the teepee. The prisoner, first of all, retired for the night. Then Big Hard Face, then White Crow went to sleep, and soon the loud snoring of Big Hard Face rattled through the lodge. Last of all, the curtain dropped before Red Wind.

Thunder Moon sat for a long time looking at the dying fire which still shot up a red hand now and again and thrust wild shadows through the teepee. He felt that he was approaching a permanence in his life. He felt that he was secure of all the future. In that security he lay down at last and slept in turn.

Physically he had done nothing the day before, but spiritually he had exhausted himself. He did not waken until the full rose of the dawn was already in the sky; did not waken until the rough hand of Big Hard Face shook him, and the voice of the chief shouted:

'Up! Up! They are gone! They are gone! White Crow, send out the alarm. Send out the searchers.'

Thunder Moon leaped up, reaching for a rifle.

'Who are gone?'

'Both! She must have set the Pawnee free. She and Rising Cloud have gone off together. . . .'

'What she?' He really did not have to ask that. Gripping at the center pole of the lodge and holding hard, he made his brain clear from the shock, made himself look back into the past. He could remember now that there had been many exchanges of glances between the two. Yet how marvelous that a woman's heart should be taken and given in silence. And to a helpless prisoner. Might it not be that his very helplessness had been the vital point of appeal to the girl?

White Crow was screeching with ugly laughter. 'I told you that the trouble would come! Now it is here, and you look sicker than an aching stomach and a bad tooth.'

He reached out and caught her. He wanted to kill her. 'Woman, devil!' he gasped at her, and stepped from the tent. Others were rushing out of every lodge entrance, gaping, chattering, and pointing toward him. Did he see smiles among them?

He raised his head and stared around at them, slowly meeting eyes, eyes and smiles that came out and then shrank before him – children, women, and proved, hardened warriors. They shrank under his eye and afterwards they would hate him for it. That he knew, but nothing mattered.

He flung a saddle on one of the chestnuts which stood beside the teepee, a glorious stallion, swift as the wind. Petted and pampered all its life, it nuzzled at his shoulder fondly now, with pricking ears, but he struck it away with a brutal blow.

'Call me a devil if you wish,' said the hard voice of White Crow behind him, 'but do not make a fool of yourself and bring back a women who detests you. She will only leave you again, or simply deceive you without leaving. This is the price, my son, of manhood.'

He listened, and looked up. The sky was brighter and more beautiful than ever before, but not for him. Only where it arched above the head of Red Wind was there beauty in it, and all the rest of the world was a draped and solemn catafalque where dead things and dead men lay. He gathered the reins, but still he delayed to leap upon the back of the horse. Perhaps White Crow was right and this was the price of manhood, paid down in pain.

# Part Two

# 17

# For Aught But Fighting

How far we travel in one moment, throwing our eyes up to a star a billion billion miles away or casting a wild thought farther still across the vast ecliptic of the soul so that in the space of a second man may be made anew! All old trails are left behind and new goals rise like faintly descried mountains.

So it was with Thunder Moon at the entrance to his lodge, gathering the reins of his horse and hesitating before he launched himself in pursuit of the woman who had left his wigwam. As White Crow had said, he was passing from youth to manhood, and the transition was an agony.

All the while his eye wandered. He saw little foolish details around him, such as a woman forcing a bolus of medicinal herbs down the throat of a dog. Into his ear would float the far off wailing of the squaws, already renewing their laments at such a distance that they seemed cataphonic waves from the horizon. He saw the sky, too, covered with a diaper design of clouds. All the while the problems of his tormented soul possessed his mind.

He looked wildly around him, striving to find some object which would win his mind away from his own torment. He found none. All that he looked on seemed detestable to him. The lodge behind him – there was none larger or finer in the tribe – was his castle and this village was his castelry. It had seemed a place spacious enough for a

man's ambitions to expand to the full and fit for the affluence of any
mind that loved power. Now it had contracted to a miserable tent set
in a huddle of wretched teepees, peopled with fools and savages.

He heard Big Hard Face arguing with White Crow inside the teepee. It was true, admitted Big Hard Face, that the woman would
make more trouble if Thunder Moon brought her back to the lodge
but still, whether she would or not, his foster son was pledged to the
father of the girl to keep her in his teepee. Find her he must – if he
could.

That seemed to solve the riddle. Act he must, or else his whole soul
would be dissolved in pain. He flung himself into the saddle. In the
scabbard running beneath his right leg was his rifle. In saddle holsters
were two heavy Colts. At his belt was his knife, but he called for his
shield and his lance. White Crow brought them, mumbling protests
still. When she saw him grasp them and sling the shield upon his back
and brandish his spear, her eyes lighted with admiration. He was far
from beautiful of face, but his sun-browned body was so alive with
power and his seat upon the stallion was so sure and easy, she felt him
to be the very beau ideal of the Indian warrior. The others who watched
him ride forth felt the same.

Instantly the legion of boys swept around him, every one of them
mounted on the fastest pony he could bag from his father's herd.

'Take pity on me, Thunder Moon!' they would beg in shrill voices.
'Take pity on me and let me ride with you. I shall fight like a man for
you. You will have all the glory. Only let me go with you. I shall make
the fires and cook and hunt for you. I shall find the trail for you. Take
pity on me, Thunder Moon.'

They rushed and swerved before him, each intent to show the skill
he possessed as a horseman, and each brandishing a weapon of some
sort. While all the rest swept back and forth, striving to catch his eye,
the son of Three Bears drifted just behind him, saying nothing, as one
who resolved that if favors were to be granted he would be close at
hand, but feeling that a boon so great should not be clamored for.

Not only did the boys beset Thunder Moon, but the finest young
warriors among the Suhtai galloped up to him, having snatched their
accoutrements and hurried toward this chance for fame. Fame there
must be, for Thunder Moon never had taken the war trail in vain.
Like a lion, he counted no coups, took no scalps, but left these glories
for those who accompanied him. The young warriors were not alone.

Here and there he could see some grim-faced, tried man of battle raising an arm in dignified salutation: 'How!' Not begging to be included in the expedition, but manifestly hungry to be invited along.

They came in this fashion to the edge of the village. Thunder Moon looked back with a solemn and sad face, very much like one who turns to take a last look at his home which he never may see again. Turning and gazing, he encountered the bright eyes of the son of Three Bears, waiting, speaking not at all, but quivering under the glance of Thunder Moon as a swift horse quivers at the touch of the whip.

The heart of the warrior was touched. He pointed to the pony which the boy mounted. 'Do you wish to go with me and on such a horse?' he asked.

The question and the almost implied invitation in it made the youngster mute for an instant, then he cried out: 'Let me come, Thunder Moon! You will see that this horse is not beautiful, but he will not fail me, and I shall not fail you.'

There was a chorus of derision from the envious. The sons of rich men in the tribe swept in short circles, displaying the matchless feet of their ponies. 'Take me, Thunder Moon! Take me! The son of Three Bears is mounted on a dog, not a horse! Take me!'

'Have you asked your father's permission?' said Thunder Moon, noticing that the boy made no reply to these taunts, but kept his wild, bright eyes fixed upon the face of the man he worshipped, as though confident that, regardless of the taunts of the others, this brave could make no fault of judgment.

'I have not asked, but his permission is given,' cried the youth.

'There stands his teepee. Come with me.'

He rode before the lodge. Out of it, as though a premonition of the question had come to him, stepped Three Bears and his single squaw. There was no more celebrated chief among the Suhtai than this man and, when all the ten tribes of the Cheyenne were gathered and their chief men in council, few were listened to more eagerly than this distinguished brave. In spite of wealth and fame, he had taken one squaw only and by her he had one son – this child who now sought to take the war path with Thunder Moon. The instant that they saw their son with the pale-faced brave, they understood the meaning. The squaw ran to her boy with a cry and tried to pull him down from his pony, chattering furiously in protest. The father, however, smiled and pretended to be happy.

'This is a great honor,' said the chief. 'I could not hope that my boy, who is yet without a name, may be taken on the war path by such a chief as Thunder Moon.'

The latter was too deeply buried in gloom to pay any heed to the compliment. He merely said: 'You are not like the tumbleweed which scatters a thousand weeds. You have only one son. Will you let him go out with me on the trail? There will be danger, Three Bears.'

'Look,' cried the squaw in a broken voice, 'you have all the boys and the young men of the Suhtai to choose from. Leave me my son!'

'I want no other than this one,' said Thunder Moon. 'I am not riding out to hunt coyotes or buffalo wolves or to get eagle feathers. This is a blood trail. I shall ride on it alone or else this boy may come with me. Of all the Suhtai he has the sharpest eye and the quickest ear. He is the swiftest on the land and the swiftest in the water. He reads the sign of the trail as though it were picture writing on the wall of his father's teepee. Tell me, Three Bears, are you content that he should go with me?'

Three Bears cast a single glance at the face of his boy and in that face he saw such a radiant fire of hope, such an eager appeal in the silence of the youth that he could only answer: 'I give him to you. Do what you will with him. If he can shoot straight when he comes home, I shall be a happy man.'

There was a sharp wail from the squaw, but Three Bears, with a single rough word, sent her with bowed head into the teepee, there to bury her fear and her sorrow.

Thunder Moon said to the boy: 'Do you know the horses of my father?'

'I have herded them and watched them. I know every name and every trick they have.'

'Which is the smallest of them all?'

'The dark-red mare which you call Sunpath.'

'Which is the most beautiful of all of our horses?'

'Sunpath also is the most beautiful.'

'Go to the lodge of Big Hard Face,' said the warrior, 'and tell him then that you will have Sunpath. Take her. Take also a good saddle and a bridle. Take ammunition and also a rifle and one of these small guns which has six voices. Take all of these things, and a good knife. My father will give you all that you require. If you see a shield that is small enough, take the shield also. When you have what you want, ride rapidly out of the village and meet me by the waterfall . . . that one with the big linn beneath it.'

Having finished these instructions, he turned and rode instantly from the village, leaving the boy almost too stunned by his good fortune to execute the commands he had received.

'Hail!' cried Three Bears, filled with exultation. 'My son rides out from our village like a great chief and not like a boy. Woman, make some pemmican ready. He will come back with a name. You shall see.'

In the meantime, Thunder Moon galloped the stallion from the village and toward that portion of the course of the river where it fell down through a group of hills and made a succession of waterfalls. While he was still at a distance, he could hear the varying voices of the cataracts, some singing high and others ominously deep and low. He listened and from far behind him he still heard the mourning cries of the Cheyenne women. How clearly it seemed proven to Thunder Moon that there was little joy and much sadness in this bitter world.

Now he reached the fall which beat into the face of a large pool and, close to the verge of the water, he sat down and the big stallion came and stood close to him. Of all the horses of Big Hard Face, there were none like Sailing Hawk for strength or for endurance. As he fled along the horizon line and over the hilltops, he had seemed often like a bird on the wing and won for himself his name.

The horse was unregarded, for Thunder Moon stared down into the pool and felt that all the future was as gloomy and dim as the surface of that broken water. He did not move until Sailing Hawk started and snorted softly. Then Thunder Moon turned his head and, across the plain, he saw coming toward him the most perfect symbol and picture of wild, free grace that ever his eyes had beheld.

Yonder flew the son of Three Bears, riding the red mare by knee-pressure alone, letting her reins fall loose, and with both his slender arms extended exultantly above his head. Upon his left arm there was a small white-faced shield. In his right hand he held a lance, not of the massive proportions of that which Thunder Moon carried, but a slender-shafted weapon as fit for throwing as for thrusting in the charge.

His long hair flying back over his shoulders, the boy raced up to Thunder Moon, whipped from the back of the mare, and dropped lightly onto his feet, standing in the attitude of one ready to receive orders.

Thunder Moon regarded him with a faint smile. One thing was certain. Unless a Pawnee bullet tagged this lad, he would never be overtaken in any battles that might lie before them. Like a god of speed incarnate was this youth. Thunder Moon, feeling old and gray before his time, pointed to a rock.

'Sit there,' he commanded. 'Before we take the trail, we must have council.' He went on with such frankness as no Indian in the world would have used, above all to a boy. 'I have lost a woman, as you know. My heart is very heavy because of her and there is a mist on my mind. I do not think lightly and easily. Now, you must think for me. Consider that somewhere on the plains all around us are a Pawnee and an Omissis girl mounted on two of the Comanche horses from my herd. In what direction they may have fled, I cannot tell. They started many, many hours ago. I have wasted much time. These horses are faster and stronger than theirs, but how can we ride them down unless we know where the trail may lie? I have considered. My mind is all empty of wisdom. Now you consider also, and let me know what to do.'

With that he dropped his head on his hand and fell again into a brown study, watching the face of the water. As for the boy, his eyes glittered with joy at being thus appealed to. His own contemplation was not done with a bowed head and a knotted brow. Instead, he turned slowly to all the quarters of the horizon, looking fixedly in each direction. Then he dropped upon one knee and, on the ground, he sketched what seemed a little map. He rose again, looked for a long moment to the southwest, leaped onto the back of Sunpath, and pointed the nose of the mare west and north.

'I am ready, master,' he said.

'I knew that you would guess at something,' said Thunder Moon. 'Do we cast in that direction? Do you think it may be there that they have fled?'

'I do more than think,' said the boy calmly. 'I know that if we ride hard, when we reach the western edge of those hills in the middle of the afternoon, the two will not yet have come out onto the plain.'

'You *know* that much? How do you know it? Keep your knowledge until we have met them. Ride first to show the way. I am too blind for anything but fighting.'

# 18

# Sparrow Hawk and Eagle

Can you imagine a little sparrow hawk, its wings hardly fledged with hard feathers, being asked by a lordly eagle to lead it to its battle and its prey? Thus it was with the son of Three Bears, conducting this mighty man of war across the prairie. All the way was not ridden in single file. Thunder Moon eventually drew up beside his youthful companion and began to talk, not so much for the sake of the boy as to banish his own troubles by the use of words. Speech can be an anodyne for many a pain, and the mind of Thunder Moon was like a house haunted by the lares and larvae of the dead. Conversation with this keen-eyed lad made a perfect lenitive and there were a score of topics at hand.

To begin with there was the equipment of the youngster. Had he handled guns before? Yes, he was proud to say that he had fired guns as much as a dozen times perhaps. What boy in the village was more familiar with their use? Thunder Moon, recalling the thousands of rounds which he had used in practice alone, could not help smiling a little. For that matter the great trouble with all Indian marksmanship was that the majority could not afford ammunition even if they possessed the weapons. Besides rifles were not like bows and arrows, things to be perfected by use in peace to prepare for times of war, they were articles of 'medicine' and rather to be prayed about than handled in ordinary times.

As they rode along, Thunder Moon gave some vigorous lessons

concerning first the mere holding of a rifle, and then its balance in the hands, how to mark with the eye before glancing through the sights, how to find the bull's-eye by letting the uncertain farther sight wobble around the target until it found dead center, how to aim a little low, and then how to squeeze the trigger with a gradual pressure so that the explosion always would come with a bit of surprise even to the firer. He showed the boy all of these things and how it is quite possible to do a very great deal of practicing without so much as discharging a gun. 'For,' he said, 'you know whether your man is dead before the bullet reaches him. You know it by the way you held the gun on the mark.'

The child listened with an almost tremulous eagerness, as a mortal would listen to a god and man in one person. When Thunder Moon allowed him to practice – not with one bullet but with a whole score of rounds – the results which the boy achieved were totally amazing. His nerves were as steady as rock and, having been taught by such a great master, he felt that to miss his target would be almost a mystery. It was not merely a lesson which he had received, it was a strong medicine which had been imparted to him and a divine power that had been entrusted to his hands.

Not rifle work only, but the more complicated practice of revolver play was also imparted, and all the details explained for the management of that true artist's weapon which should be fired rather by sense of touch than by sense of sight. As for the knife and the spear, the boy already could handle them with a sinister skill, and he could wield the shield and the lance together like a tried warrior.

They prepared for war as they crossed the plains, but all the talk was not on the side of Thunder Moon. If he could teach in some respects, he could learn in others.

'Tell me,' he said, 'what sign are you following?'

His own eyes could detect no print on sand or in grass as they rode.

'No sign,' replied the boy.

'How then,' asked Thunder Moon a little sharply, 'did you learn where to look for these two? By medicine?'

'No,' said the boy. 'Where would they go when they left the camp? That was what I asked myself. I stood and stared around at the edge of the sky. Shall I tell you what I thought of?'

'Yes, tell me everything.'

'They would not leave until very late, after the last sounds had died in the village.'

'That is true.'

'The squaws were crying until very late.'

'Yes.'

'Then, when these two slipped out from the camp, they had to steal two horses, and they took ones from your Comanche band.'

'That is true.'

'Which took a great deal of time.'

'Perhaps.'

'When at last they were on their horses, they were not like ordinary prisoners escaping. If they had been, they would have ridden straight back to the Pawnee village.'

'Why would they not ride in that direction?'

'Because it was already late and they knew that before long in the dawn light Thunder Moon would come running after them on his great tall horse, eating up the ground like a fire or like an eagle swooping out of the sky. They were afraid and they looked around then, I think, and said to themselves that quickly they must get off the face of the plains so open . . . like the palm of a hand . . . and, if they were seen, they would be destroyed. How could they escape from Thunder Moon, once his eyes found them?'

Thunder Moon looked at the boy seriously, but he found no mockery in the eyes of the youngster.

'They saw,' went on the youth, 'the low line of the shadows to the north and the east and they told themselves that first they would gallop straight for those hills and pray to get to them before the morning light began. After that, they would turn and ride around behind the hills, or through them toward the village of the Pawnee. This, I think, is the truth, and we should come to them not long after they leave the valleys of the hills and ride out into the open. May it be true! May Tarawa keep me from speaking a lie to you.'

He said it most fervently and Thunder Moon, amazed by this exhibition of logic, was silent for a time.

'What is it that sees most quickly of all the things that run on the plains?'

'The antelope,' answered the boy.

'What is it that hears most quickly?'

'The antelope also, when it pricks up its long ears and stands to listen.'

'No ears are quicker than yours and no eyes are sharper on the whole prairie,' said Thunder Moon gravely, 'for you see and hear partly with eyes and ears and partly with your own hidden mind. Therefore I shall call you Standing Antelope, but never until you have counted coup on a Pawnee.'

It threw the boy into a strong ecstasy, though as usual he controlled his emotion and said not a word. For a long time afterward his eyes were glistening with pleasure and he could not keep a shadow of a smile from the corners of his mouth.

They were passing now through a sea of grass, not very long, but growing thick and soft, an ideal fodder, and the buffalo were sure to know of such an ideal pasture. In fact, little groups of them were seen here and there, the outlying members of some herd that wandered farther to the west.

The boy would have passed them by. His heart was bent on the great things to be done. When they came upon a little swale, with a great bull standing in the center of it, Thunder Moon said: 'Have you ever killed a bull?'

'I have killed one calf,' said the boy regretfully, 'and no more.'

'The rifle is loaded. Ride down into the hollow and kill that bull.'

One excited and grateful glance was flashed toward him and, instantly, Sunpath was flying into the swale toward the monster buffalo, like a red arrow from the string. The bull, wheeling, made off at full gallop. For all his clumsiness, the buffalo can gallop at an amazing speed, but the red mare was alongside very quickly, the rifle was leveled and fired, and at the single shot the bull dropped its head, turned a complete somersault, and lay still.

Here was a thing worth narrating at the fire. What other boy of all the Cheyennes had slain a bull at a single stroke? The son of Three Bears was beside himself with joy, yet even then he remembered his manners and stood aside to let his elder dispose of the carcass. Thunder Moon, however, reined his stallion nearby and said simply: 'It is your bull. Take what parts you wish. We shall have fresh meat tonight. You have done well. Remember that the bullet which kills a buffalo will kill a Pawnee also.'

The boy took the tongue and then, with an expert knife, he removed a few portions of the choice part of the haunch. They had not time to take the hide, of course. In another moment they were swinging across the prairie again.

There was a difference, however. They had been man and boy before. Now they were like man and man, for the youngster had proved his weapons and confidence was in his heart.

It was late afternoon when they reached the edge of the hills on the western end of their range. Here Thunder Moon made a halt in the shadow of a rock ledge and loosed the cinches of the saddles so that the horses could breathe. He and the boy lay among the upper rocks to watch. The sun was hot, but hotter than the sun was the heart of Thunder Moon as he stared over the waves of grassland and waited. Even so, for all his eagerness, it was not he who had the first view of the quarry, but the soft voice of the boy murmured: 'Ha! They have come.'

He saw them then, a gray horse and a brown issuing from the shadows of the hills and striking at a trot into the open country. The girl was mounted on the brown; on the gray rode Rising Cloud, the Pawnee.

'They are mine,' said Thunder Moon in his savage heart of hearts, and instantly they returned to the horses, drew up the cinches, and rode out into the open lands.

Their horses had not made a dozen strides when they were sighted by the fugitives and, as pigeons scatter when the hawk flies toward them, so the girl turned and sped back toward the hills while the Pawnee darted straight ahead.

First Thunder Moon let his heart lead him and swerved toward the girl, but then rage mastered him and he pointed the head of the stallion toward the gray horse of Rising Cloud.

# 19

# A Fallen Cloud

A stern chase is a proverbially long one at sea. By land it is not much shorter if the course is laid upon the open prairie and the horses are in any degree fairly matched. In this case they were not matched. Tough and true were all those Comanche ponies which Thunder Moon had stolen in the hot southland, but never for a moment could the striding of those shorter legs match the long gallop of the chestnuts. Like an eagle, with a strong wing-stroke, ran the stallion. Like a rapid hawk beside him flew the mare with the boy erect and joyous in the saddle. With every moment the distance that separated the hunter and the hunted grew less and less.

Rising Cloud twice wheeled in the saddle and discharged his rifle at his pursuers – well-aimed bullets they were and, as they were fired, Thunder Moon turned his head a little and regarded the boy. The son of Three Bears merely shouted with joy as he raced battle-fire for the first time – laughed and shouted and urged the swift mare to greater efforts until even Sailing Hawk, weighted as he was by the vastly greater bulk of his rider, hardly could keep pace with the smaller horse.

The stolen pony on which the Pawnee rode, however, was beaten by superior speed, not mastered in endurance and, to the last stride, he continued to fly across the prairie with head and tail straight as a string in the greatness of his effort.

Once more Rising Cloud slewed himself around in the middle to take aim, and now they were at hardly more than half a pistol shot away. It would be madness to endure that point-blank discharge. So Thunder Moon snatched a revolver from its holster and fired quickly. The gun exploded in the hand of Rising Cloud, but the bullet sped at random and he swayed heavily to one side, reeled, and almost fell.

'He is gone!' screamed the son of Three Bears. 'He is dying!' Giving wings to the mare, he closed in on the enemy with a burst of speed that threw him ahead of Thunder Moon. Rising Cloud had snatched up the lance with which, as well as with the fallen rifle, he had been equipped. Through his right shoulder the bullet of Thunder Moon had passed, and blood was spurting over that side of his body; but in his left hand he balanced the spear and thrust sharply with it at the Suhtai lad, at the same time swerving his pony to the side and shouting his war cry.

There was no trace of the craven in this Pawnee. He intended to die fighting gloriously. His first stroke was toward the boy. The son of Three Bears dipped on the back of the mare and, striking up the weapon of the Pawnee, he pressed in and smote the half naked body of Rising Cloud with his clenched fists.

'So I count coup! I count first coup! I count it!' screamed the boy, as the charge of the mare swept him past and out of the reaches of danger.

For that matter, Rising Cloud had a greater task on his hands than the defense needed against a child. The most terrible warrior in all the hosts of the Cheyennes, those ferocious horsemen, now swept down upon him. When he saw that the Pawnee possessed no gun with which to fight but had to defend himself with the spear alone, Thunder Moon had thrust his revolver into the holster – the rifle he never had touched – and taking his lance he closed on the Pawnee. His own spear gripped in his unskillful left hand, the Pawnee could not withstand this attack for an instant. His weapon was beaten aside by a cunning of lance-craft as great as a rapier parry and then, dropping the spear, Thunder Moon grappled his foe in his bare hands.

The boy had swerved on the mare as rapidly as a bird on the wing and, rushing back with spear ready to thrust the Pawnee through and through, he withheld his hand with a shout when he saw Rising Cloud torn from his saddle and instantly mastered in the Herculean grip of Thunder Moon.

Vainly the Pawnee brave writhed and struggled. His right arm hung helpless. Even had he possessed his full might of hand, it seemed that he could not have fought against this giant for a moment. For like a giant the other seemed, at least in the eyes of the son of Three Bears.

Now, bleeding and disarmed, Rising Cloud lay on the ground and the Suhtai warrior had dropped on one knee beside him, knife poised. He grasped the fallen brave by the scalp lock and holding him thus securely, he looked up to the broad, bright sky above him where the sunset color was just beginning.

'Sky People,' he said, 'if I give you this man as a sacrifice, be kind to me and teach me what to do with the woman.' He looked down at the Pawnee.

'Why should you kill me, Thunder Moon?' asked the victim.

'You have murdered the Suhtai. You have been sheltered in my lodge from the women who wanted to torment you. Then you have stolen a woman from me and ridden away with her. Are those reasons, Pawnee wolf?'

'The Suhtai I fought with were killed in the open field,' answered the Pawnee. 'You kept me from the hands of the squaws in your camp and for that I thank you. As for the woman, it is more true that she stole me away than that I stole her.'

'That is a lie and the gray father of lies,' said Thunder Moon.

'It is the truth,' said the captive. 'How could I have escaped if she had not cut the rope that held me fast? But she cut the rope and whispered to me to follow her. When we were outside, she gave me a gun and a lance and a knife. I told her that she had better go back into the lodge. . . .'

'Even the snake that twists through the grass at least speaks truth when it speaks,' said Thunder Moon, 'but you are not honest. I think that all your heart is full of wrong talk. You loved this girl of the Omissis and you made her love you and stole away with her. . . .'

'If I were the head chief of the Pawnees,' said the captive, 'then I should take her into my lodge because there is no other woman in the prairies who is like her. Since I am not the head chief, I shall have nothing to do with her.'

'That is a likely story,' said Thunder Moon with a sneer. 'When you were outside my lodge with her, you told her to go back?'

'I told her that one of us might escape from you, but that no woman could flee across the prairies as fast as you would pursue.'

'She would not listen to you? She loved you so much that she would have to go with you?'

'She didn't love me, but she would rather have fled away with an owl or a buzzard than stay in your teepee and become your squaw.'

At this the knife quivered in the grip of Thunder Moon, but he held himself from striking with an effort that made his neck muscles bulge.

# 20

# A Pawnee Warrior

The Pawnee, in the meantime, regarded his captor gravely and steadily.
Thunder Moon stood up and began to walk back and forth, full of his
thoughts. Sometimes he paused, determined to slay the Pawnee at
once in sacrifice to the Sky People. Then again he felt an overwhelm-
ing need to know the truth about Red Wind and whatever she had
said to her Pawnee companion.

He said to the boy: 'Help to stop the bleeding of his shoulder. Wash
that wound and tie it so that it will bleed no more.'

The wound was dressed with the rough and quick skill which all
Indians possessed in such matters. Then Thunder Moon came back to
the captive, saying: 'Tell me, what is Red Wind that she detests me?
Where has she found a richer Indian? Who has killed more enemies?
Who rides on swifter horses or has a bigger herd? Who keeps more
guns in his lodge and who has many pounds of ammunition and who
has such stacks of the softest buffalo robes?'

'Can a woman marry a horse, a gun, or a buffalo robe?' replied the
Pawnee.

'Pawnee coward! Creeping, sneaking, skunk-bear!' cried Thunder
Moon in a wild fury, 'do you dare to tell me that she answered you
that way?'

'Why should I tell you any more?' asked Rising Cloud. 'You call
me by many evil names and you will not believe me. Besides, you are

about to sacrifice me and send my spirit up to attend the Sky People. Why should I talk before I die? No, you may go to Red Wind and ask her all of these same questions.'

'There are ways, however, of making men talk,' said Thunder Moon, with a devilish smile.

'There are ways,' said the Pawnee, meeting the eye of his captor firmly, 'but you will not use them.'

'I shall not?' cried the Suhtai chief.

'Because you jump when you hear the cry of a child and you will not so much as lift a scalp. You have no heart for torture, Thunder Moon!'

The big man glowered at his prisoner, but he said nothing for a moment. The Pawnee sat composed, cross-legged on the prairie, his face already becoming grave and dignified like one about to receive his death and meet it in the best manner possible.

The son of Three Bears ventured to speak. His nostrils had flared wide and then contracted again.

'Why should Thunder Moon trouble himself with such work? Let Thunder Moon go away and ride on the prairie. When he comes back, he will find that this man will be ready to talk of anything that is asked.'

Thunder Moon waved him away. 'This is a man and not a sick coyote,' he said. 'You could tear him to pieces by little bits. You could send birds to tear him and devour him, but still he would not speak after he has once locked his teeth.'

There was a glitter of pleasure in the eyes of the Pawnee as he heard this compliment, spoken unwillingly.

'But your speech may be bought,' suggested Thunder Moon.

'What price do you pay to a dead man?' asked the Pawnee. 'How many robes and guns and horses will you pay to a man before you sacrifice him?'

'I could kill you,' said Thunder Moon, 'by the hand of that boy and let him scalp you and take your medicine bag. Your spirit would be doomed to dwindle and die like a whistle on the wind.'

'It is true,' said the Pawnee, his face unmoved no matter what desolation was in his heart.

'But suppose that I promise you an honorable burial with your weapons beside you and I kill that horse so that your spirit may ride it in the other world? Is that a price that would make you talk?'

'What would make me sure that you would do these things?' asked the Pawnee anxiously.

'My honor and my promise,' said Thunder Moon.

'We have made many treaties and had many promises from the Cheyennes,' said the Pawnee darkly, 'and what has become of them? They went away in the wind like dust.'

Thunder Moon drew himself up to his height. 'I am not a boy,' he said. 'I have not spent my life in my lodge, like a woman. I have spoken in the council. Also I have ridden on the war path. When has Thunder Moon failed to make his word good?'

The Pawnee reflected. 'That is true,' he admitted at last.

Silence fell between them.

'It is a great price,' said Thunder Moon suddenly, 'to pay in order to know what words a woman spoke. But I shall pay one still higher. I remember that you have sat in my lodge and eaten meat from the meat pot and slept there. Your voice has been heard in my teepee. Therefore I cannot hate you, Rising Cloud. You are a Pawnee, but I think that you are a good man. Some day I may meet you in battle at the side of your brother. Then perhaps the Sky People will give me strength to kill you both. But now I shall give you your life and that rifle to carry back to your people, and that horse so that you may go back not as a beggar but as a warrior who has escaped with honor from a great danger. If that price seems enough to you, tell me everything that passed between you and the woman, and leave out nothing.'

The Pawnee was schooled, like all Indians, to control his emotions stiffly when in the presence of strangers. Above all, he knew how to guard himself when he was with an enemy. But now he could not help a quick exclamation of wonder. He looked at Thunder Moon. He looked past that hero to the boy and saw the son of Three Bears writhing with rage and disappointment.

'You have spoken,' said the Pawnee.

'The Sky People may hear me!' said Thunder Moon.

'That is not necessary,' replied the Pawnee. 'For it is true that all men know the honor of Thunder Moon is not the honor of a wolf or a snake. Now I shall tell you everything. When I sat in your tent and the woman was brought in by her father, I looked at her and saw that she was beautiful. I have seen many young women in many tribes, but none like her. I thought that her father was anxious to get rid of her because she was wicked. Why else should he send her away and pay such a great price to the man who would take her into his teepee even without making her his wife? So I thought that perhaps I might be able to talk to her and make her my friend and then escape through her. I looked at her when I could. I smiled at her. It was like smiling at the painted bear on your father's lodge. She would not see me. So I was a great deal surprised when in the darkness of last night she came to me and cut the rope that tied me.

'We went softly outside the lodge and she gave me the weapons, as I told you. Then, as I have said, I urged her to stay at the lodge because she could not escape with me. But she would not stay. She gave me a reason for it.'

'What reason, then?' asked Thunder Moon.

'She said that you are a paleface and that therefore some day you will go back to your tribe. Tarawa would pour sorrow on the heart of any Indian maiden who married you.'

'Pawnee,' said Thunder Moon sternly, 'it is true that my skin is not as dark as yours, but still it is not white. Some men are dark and some are light. Snake-That-Talks is almost black, but who says that he is not a Cheyenne. As for me, no one but a fool and the son of a fool would think that I am not a Suhtai. I am the son of Big Hard Face. Is not he a Suhtai? Have I not been known these many years as a Cheyenne? Or is my life a dream?'

'I hear you and I understand you,' said the Pawnee in rather a gentle voice, 'but I know that I have seen white men at the trading forts. Some of them are very white. Some are brown from living in the sun. You are like those brown ones. You are not like a Suhtai in your looks or in your ways. You are not like any Pawnee, or like any Sioux or Comanche that I have seen. So I believed the woman when she told me these things. She did not want to stay in your lodge and become your squaw.'

Thunder Moon bowed his head. He felt more crushed with sorrow than if he had been told of the death of a good friend.

'I could not persuade her to stay there,' went on the Pawnee. 'I asked her what she wanted to do, and if she would be a squaw to me when she came to the Pawnees. But she said that she did not want that. She only wanted me to help her get away. Afterwards she would think what she would do. When I heard this, I talked no more. It was dangerous to crouch there in the dark, talking. So I went with her to the place where your Comanche horses were. We stole two of them. We led them a little way off. Then we put on them the saddles that we had taken from our teepee. We rode away. I cannot tell how you found our trail, unless the Sky People sent a spirit to sit on your shoulder and tell you how to ride.'

Thunder Moon looked at the boy. There was triumph in the eye of the latter, but no boast upon his lips.

'It is the son of Three Bears who read your mind,' said the warrior. 'All that passes on the prairies, he sees. All the sounds that come down the wind, he hears. He is like the standing antelope. That is his name. When you go back to your people, tell them that the Suhtai have a new warrior, who is young but very wise. His name is Standing Antelope.'

'I shall remember him,' said the Pawnee, his eyes narrowing a little with menace and malice. 'Now, Thunder Moon, am I free?'

'You are free. Take the horse and all that you carried away from my tent. Go back to your people, Rising Cloud.'

The latter, in silence, secured the Comanche pony, sprang onto its back, and then darted off at full gallop. He did not pass straight away, however, but swung around in a short circle and came back before Thunder Moon.

'Listen to me,' said the Pawnee. 'Spotted Bull is no friend of yours. But he has spoken the truth. There is bad medicine in Red Wind. Leave her trail. Let her go and disappear on the prairie like a small cloud when it rises in the sky on a very bright and hot day. She will bring no happiness into your teepee.'

'Tell me,' said Thunder Moon, 'what have you learned that makes you sure of all of these things?'

'How does one learn about the eagle?' asked the Pawnee brave. 'By watching it fly! How does one learn the squirrel? By seeing its ways in the trees. How does one learn the mountain lion? By following its tracks. That is how I have learned about her. No man ever can be happy with her.'

'I am not blind,' said Thunder Moon. 'Already I have sat in the same teepee with her. But I see nothing wrong about her. My mind is filled with mist when I hear you say these things. I cannot tell why her father wanted to send her away from his lodge. Why should he hate her?'

The Pawnee listened, frowning with thought. At length he said: 'I shall tell you only one thing. Her father does not hate her. No, no! But he is terribly afraid of her. That is why he sent her away, because he saw that if she remained in his lodge much longer, he could not remain the head chief of the Omissis.'

'You answer one riddle by telling me another,' said Thunder Moon. 'What do you mean by this? Why cannot he remain the head chief of the Omissis if she remains in his lodge?'

'I have given you my last answer,' said the Pawnee. 'My arm swells and the fever will begin soon, and I have a long distance to ride. Farewell, brother. Bad fortune may come to you and yet you never will lose two friends among the Pawnees.'

With this he wheeled his horse again and, this time, he did not return but headed across the vast prairie where he soon diminished almost to a point that seemed to waver up and down with the heat lines that rose from the surface of the plains.

# 21

# What Is Glory?

Thunder Moon, after watching the retreating brave for a moment, turned to the newly-named warrior at his side, and the boy cried eagerly to him: 'You have given life to that lying Pawnee. You have kept your promise. Now let me ride after him. He has only one arm, but he is older and stronger than I am. Let me try to catch him. It will be my first scalp and I may count coup on him again.'

'I cannot give a thing and take back my gift again,' said Thunder Moon, smiling a little. 'He could not escape from you. His pony is fast and tough, but Sunpath is tougher and stronger. She would be up with him in a very short time, of course, and then you would have no trouble in killing a man who has not a bit of strength in his wise right hand. Tell me, Standing Antelope . . . is there any glory in killing a helpless man?'

'Why is there not?' asked the boy.

'Begin on the back trail that will lead us to the Omissis girl,' said Thunder Moon. 'As we go, tell me what glory comes from destroying a man who cannot fight back against you?'

They rode side by side through the grass, swinging at a swift gallop toward that rift in the hills into which the girl had disappeared when she had turned away from the Pawnee who had accompanied her.

'Are the Pawnees our friends or our enemies?' asked the youth in counter-question.

'They are our enemies,' admitted Thunder Moon, smiling at the idea that they might be any other thing.

'If they are enemies,' went on Standing Antelope, thinking hard as he rode, 'then every boy may grow into a warrior who will hunt us. Every little girl will become a squaw and raise children and teach them to hunt for our scalps. And every wounded brave someday will be healthy and strong again, and then he will ride out to kill us. For all of these reasons, my Father, we must kill the Pawnees, young or old or sick, and take their scalps, and count coups upon them.'

'So you say,' said Thunder Moon, 'but how is it that even the old men are to be killed, and the old women? They have passed the time when they could do us any harm.'

'On this earth, yes,' said the boy instantly, 'but not in the sky where the spirits of the warriors chase the ghosts of the buffalo. There we want to go and live with the good Cheyennes and be happy together, but certainly we could not be happy there if the spirits of the Pawnees went up there in great numbers. So we must kill them all, if we can, so that our ghosts will not be bothered in the life with Tarawa, where the sun always is shining.'

Thunder Moon smiled a little at this enthusiastic and bloody argument, but he did not reply to it. For his part, he had no desire to mix in any purposeless slaughter. War was to him a glorious game and, like a game, he played it with all the strength of his hands and with all the cunning of his mind, but always obeying certain instincts of fair play that checked him short of the thoroughgoing methods of the Suhtai. A well-laid ambuscade was to them the height of good policy and clever fighting. To kill from behind was much better than to kill from the front, for he who killed in perfect safety showed not only the superiority of his strength and medicine, but also the superiority of his wit. Accordingly, to be merciful was to be a fool. As for the crowning joy of meeting a strong enemy face to face and battling for the supremacy, it was to the Suhtai a sort of barbarous and mad pleasure. Upon Thunder Moon they looked as upon a barbarous and half insane warrior, useful certainly in the battle, deadly beyond belief with his weapons, but totally wild in his methods.

These were the thoughts which, as Thunder Moon could guess, were now passing behind the brow of his young companion. For his own part, he said nothing. He had learned from bitter experience even in the lodge of Big Hard Face that his thoughts were not the thoughts of his tribe, just as his strength was not theirs, and their strength was not his.

He was silent for another and far graver reason. It was because he wanted to turn in his mind the words which the Omissis girl had spoken to the Pawnee. She had called Thunder Moon himself a white man! For that reason she did not want to remain in his lodge. The blood of Thunder Moon grew hot with anger.

As for a trifling matter of lightness in color, what was that? Very gladly would he have had his skin a copper red. But since that could not be, he was certain that in his heart he was a good Suhtai, devoted to the interests of the tribe. As for being a white man – a white man indeed! From hot his blood ran cold.

He had had glimpses of those people. Strangely, stiffly dressed unless they attempted an awkward imitation of Indian freedom of costume, they moved out onto the prairie, trading for furs, quarreling with one another, making cunning bargains, loving money with a detestable greed, cheating their customers, avoiding the war path as long as they could, blind upon the trail, deceitful in their councils, aimlessly chattering with one another or sullenly silent. They were only worth attention because, so the wisest chiefs said, behind those white people there was a mysterious power, and in their hands there was medicine of strange strength, so that sometimes ten of them, standing shoulder to shoulder, might beat off a hundred Indian enemies. But place one white man on the plains, and even an Indian boy like Standing Antelope could account for him and bring in his scalp before many days of trailing had ended.

Such was the white man – such was his meaning to Thunder Moon. No wonder that his lip curled with scorn and disgust when he heard that the Omissis girl had placed him in the category of these disgusting people, these strange, unpleasant creatures. No wonder also that the girl, thinking such thoughts of him, should wish to leave his teepee, even with a man she found a captive there. She had fled away as from a curse. Now he wanted with a ten-fold desire to find her, let her know the error of her thoughts, and so, bring her happily back to his lodge.

Afterward, he would see to it that his skin should be darkened with certain stains of which he knew. Yes, he would make himself a figure of flaming red if necessary, so that foolish thoughts might not come into the mind of the spectator – into the mind of Red Wind, above all!

He pushed forward vigorously and Sailing Hawk answered with a mighty stride that devoured the ground before them. They entered the shadowed mouth of the valley into which the girl had gone. Instead of going straight up the hollow, young Standing Antelope – transfigured even in the eyes of Thunder Moon by the name which he now wore and by the coup which he had so lately counted – rode up to the top of the left-hand ridge. He then swung down from it and crossed hastily to the opposite height and, then with a wild war cry, raced straight down the ridge and toward the open plains beyond.

Thunder Moon followed, thinking that the boy must be mad but, as he gained the mouth of the valley, he saw the brown pony racing sturdily over the plain, and the girl jockeying her mount along with a skill which no brave could have surpassed.

He shook his head as he loosed the reins of Sailing Hawk. How like a fox she was! For his own part, he would have pushed deep into the hills on her trail. When he finally solved the trail problem, it would have led him back to the prairies onto which she had doubled.

He could thank Standing Antelope for this day's work and, in his heart, he vowed that instant that he would make the lad a present of all the weapons which he carried on that day. He sent Sailing Hawk after the fugitive.

She rode well, but she rode not well enough. Young Standing Antelope rode well also, but he could not rival the wild speed with which the stallion now plunged ahead, inspired by his rider. Past Standing Antelope went Thunder Moon, as though the boy were indeed standing. The girl drew back toward him. It seemed that the short-legged pony was laboring upon a treadmill, so swiftly did the stallion overtake it, and Thunder Moon, as he drew near, saw the girl turn her frightened head and glance back.

Exultation filled him. His war cry burst from his lips. His shadow fell upon her. The next instant his mighty arm had swept her from the saddle.

# 22

# Standing Antelope Becomes a Man

So slender and graceful had she seemed on the horse, so delicately light, that as he reached for her, he half felt that the power of his grip would crush her. But, behold, it was like grappling with a muscular man. Tense and swift she whirled upon him and a knife flashed in her hand and hovered at his throat. With desperate speed he clutched the knife-hand, and the weapon fell from her numbed fingers. Sailing Hawk came to a halt, and Thunder Moon let his captive drop lightly to her feet.

Standing Antelope galloped the mare behind the girl and remained stiffly alert in the saddle, spear in hand.

'Do not trust her, my Father,' he said. 'I saw her try her teeth on you. Tarawa made her hand slow or else she would have murdered you and then I should have had to kill her. It is an evil thing when a Cheyenne kills a Cheyenne. She-wolf! Little mountain lion! Remember that I am standing here behind you.'

Thunder Moon dismounted slowly and then waved the boy aside.

'Go catch the pony,' he said to his ally. 'Then keep away for a little. I wish to talk.'

'That is how she makes medicine . . . with her talk,' said the boy. 'Do not trust yourself near her, my Father.'

He received no answer from his leader, who stood looking down at the girl in fascinated silence. So Standing Antelope withdrew and, as he rode away toward the Comanche pony, which still struggled on with a tired gallop, he kept his head turned and watched this odd pair – the man so massive in his power, the girl so slenderly made but with her dauntless head flung up.

It could not be said that she was merely hostile. She was more or less than that. She rather looked at Thunder Moon with fear mixed with some other emotion which he could not understand. He touched his throat, where the flesh still tingled as though the knife had pricked him there.

'Red Wind,' he said gravely, 'do you know what is done among the Suhtai when a woman takes a weapon and turns it against her man?'

She was silent.

'She is tied to a post of the lodge and then she is whipped until her back bleeds.'

The girl did not wince.

'And afterwards?' she said.

'Afterwards she is turned loose and thrust from the village with her feet bare and no food and no weapon to save herself and made to wander across the prairie until she dies, or until she finds some wandering group of warriors which will take her off with them if they see fit.'

'Turn me free then without a horse or weapon or moccasins,' said the girl, 'and whip me first until the blood runs down my back.'

Thunder Moon winced. 'That would be easier for you,' he suggested bitterly, 'than to return to my lodge with me?'

Words may be bullets at times, but silence is a pointed gun, full of awful suggestion. She was silent again.

'I understand you,' said Thunder Moon, the blood passing into his face. 'You would rather be left to starve than to come back with me. I am like a sick dog to you, hateful when I am near you.'

She kept her large, grave eyes upon him and still said nothing. He wondered at her, for her expression was perfectly masked and not the slightest shadow of feeling appeared there.

In the other days, when she first came to his teepee, he had felt that her features were too immobile. But when she had swerved upon him as he seized her today, he had changed his mind. Never had fear or despair been more eloquently shown than it was then in her face.

'All is well,' said Thunder Moon sadly and angrily. 'You would knife me like a Pawnee. Yes, you would kill me far sooner than you would kill a Pawnee.' A new thought came into his mind and startled him. 'Why was it,' he said, 'that when you had snatched your knife, and when my hands were busied with the reins and with holding your body...why was it then that you did not drive home the knife in my throat?'

There was a change in her then. A sudden start, and a sort of shadow that fled across her eyes. It was gone at once but he knew that, in some manner, he had disturbed her composure.

'I understand, however,' he went on, as the explanation came to him, 'and the truth is that you would have plunged the knife into my body, except that you knew that afterward there would be a terrible accounting with Standing Antelope. Tell the truth. Be brave and tell me that that is the truth.'

She merely watched him, calmly, without expression. Almost like a polite person listening to the babble of a child, eager to have the noise cease, but not wishing to hurt the feelings of the youngster. Thunder Moon felt reproved and abashed when not a single sharp word had been spoken to him.

'Mount your horse,' he said, pointing to the pony which Standing Antelope, in the meantime, had captured and brought back to them. 'Mount your horse and be sure that for my part I should not bother to bring you back to the lodge of my father. I should not wish to keep you, but would let you wander over the prairies wheresoever you might choose. Only my promise to your father holds me. Do you believe that?'

'No,' said the girl

The monosyllable threw him back on his heels and totally unbalanced his strength of self-content. He looked at her more narrowly. Yet she did not speak with the edged tongue of an insolent woman, seeking for an opportunity to inflict pain. Rather, she was watching him with thought, and filled with a quiet contemplation.

Thunder Moon felt his strength slip from him. He was about to slip back into the common resource of all men who feel themselves weakening and fly into a fit of temper, when a soft puff of wind came over the prairie, making the grass flash under its feet, and bringing to the warrior a delicate fragrance, as though some rare pomatum had been used to dress the hair of the girl. That wind blew through his soul and carried his anger away with it.

He let the girl mount without any reproof from him and he, in turn, leaped into the saddle on Sailing Hawk. Then he waved the girl ahead and he followed with Standing Antelope. His anger began to return again, for why should the girl have been so sure that he had another reason for bringing her back to his lodge? What other reason, really, did he have? To take as his squaw an unwilling girl was a depth of cruelty and folly quite beneath him, and yet he felt that she was right. There was some other motive that impelled him. To face the loss of Red Wind would have been harder than to see all his other goods in the world destroyed before his eyes.

'She does not sing sorrow,' observed Standing Antelope, gravely approving of the erect carriage of the girl as she rode before them.

Thunder Moon made no answer. He was growing more and more irritable and poor Sailing Hawk had to pay tollage for the troubled spirit of his master. The stallion made a side leap in passing a small hole in the ground and Thunder Moon cut him shrewdly with his whip and then reined in the charger with a wicked violence.

The boy observed and contained his disgust for a moment, but finally could stand it no longer. 'When a dog is beaten, there is a woman in the lodge,' he quoted from folk lore tales.

'Why do you say that?' asked Thunder Moon, turning his frown on his young companion.

'Because I see that you are angry,' said the boy, 'and I know that you cannot be angry with Sailing Hawk.'

The warrior said sternly: 'You have done well today, Standing Antelope. You have hunted down a hard trail. You have brought me to the enemy. You attacked him bravely. You have a reward. You have counted a coup and won a name. Beyond that, I give you the rifle and the revolver you carry, and the knife and the lance, and the saddle. Now you may ride out as a warrior. But more than all this, I give you strong advice. Do not speak before your elders until your opinion is asked.'

Under this rebuke the boy winced, but he maintained his new dignity with a rare determination, saying: 'Oh, Thunder Moon, the word of a friend is better to me than the counting of twenty coups or a herd of a hundred horses. I cannot take these gifts from you.'

'Do I have to beg a child to take what I offer him?' exclaimed Thunder Moon, flying into a greater rage.

The boy looked at him with great wonder. This passion seemed to him utterly childish. And being a boy in his own person, he was amazed at this lack of dignity in the hero beside him. For nothing is more quickly seen by a child than a touch of folly in his elders.

'You have offered me rich gifts,' said the boy gently, 'but you have taken away your kindness to me at the same time. I do not want to make the exchange.'

'It is true! It is true!' said Thunder Moon, recovering instantly from his fury. 'I am like a sinew-shrunk old horse and I stumble as I go. If I took my heart away from you, Standing Antelope, I give it to you again, and all the arms and the other gifts with it. I have lost my temper like an old squaw!'

Tears of joy stood in the eyes of Standing Antelope as the warrior made this confession, and his young breast heaved suddenly. He had to look quickly away for a moment before he could trust himself and, when he spoke again to his older friend, it was with such a smile as comes from the very heart of a man.

'You have taught me how to be a man,' said the boy. 'You have let me count my first coup on a man you had made helpless. Now you have filled my hands with weapons. No brave among the Suhtai will be so envied as Standing Antelope. But ah, my Father, the rest is as nothing to me, now that all is well between us.'

# 23

# The Difference

All through the day, the interest of Thunder Moon in this child had been growing, and now it increased with a sudden bound. Looking at the boy he knew that this was the high and pure strain of Indian blood which furnished the tribes with their great chiefs – great in war and great in council, not mere seekers for blood and scalps, but leaders of their nations. He was seeing at its fountainhead the pure stream which would one day be a mighty current.

He said to the boy, with a smile: 'You are wise, Standing Antelope.'

'Father,' said Standing Antelope, 'if I had been blind, still I could have told that the woman had angered you by your voice as you spoke to Sailing Hawk.'

'How could you tell that?'

'I have heard you talk to him as if he were a man. All the Suhtai know how you go out into the pastures to visit him, and how he comes running when he sees you, and how he guards you through the herds of the horses. We have seen how he trembles for joy when you spring on his back. The warriors say that even battle he loves less than he loves his master.'

Thunder Moon, soothed by this speech, passed his hand along the shining neck of the stallion, and the big horse tipped his head a little to look back at his rider, and his step which had been smooth before became as light as the wind.

'Why should the woman anger me?' said Thunder Moon. 'I have found her and brought her back. I have beaten the man with whom she ran away. Since I do not want her for my squaw, but only to keep her in my lodge as I promised her father, therefore why should I be angered?'

At this the other squinted at the form of the girl, and shook his head. 'I do not know,' he said at last. 'I only know that my father has said that women and mules require strong hands. Perhaps you are too kind to the Omissis maiden? She gives you no answer for your kindness except a blank eye like the eye of a dying buffalo. That may be what angers you.'

Thunder Moon talked no more of this subject. They had skirted the hills to the south and now, voyaging over the plains, they came in sight of the distant lights of the village. The evening had thickened about them as they journeyed. At the same time, they reached a little run of water and a group of low trees.

There Thunder Moon halted. He could have pressed on into the village at once but, for a reason which he himself did not understand in the least, he wished to delay that return. They soon had a fire blazing – a fire of a reckless height, for it might attract the attention of any prowling bands of horse thieves such as were forever wandering near the limits of the Cheyenne encampment. In the fire the girl roasted the meat which Standing Antelope gave her.

She accepted it without a word. Without a word she cooked it. When it was roasted to a turn, she gave all to the two men and retired a little.

The boy, starved by his day's work, instantly was devouring the roasted bits with avidity. Thunder Moon ate more slowly. Suddenly he said: 'Maiden, you also are hungry. Come nearer to the fire. Take the meat and eat.'

Standing Antelope exclaimed: 'Is it fit for a woman to eat in the presence of warriors, Father?'

'Then go sit by yourself in the dark,' said Thunder Moon impatiently.

'He has spoken the truth,' said the girl as Standing Antelope, his dignity much outraged, picked up a portion of the meat and retired with it.

'Whatever he has spoken,' said Thunder Moon, 'it is my pleasure to have you come to the fire and eat.'

She came closer to the fire and sat down, cross-legged. Yet still she was half in the darkness, and the massive, metal-red braids of her hair glistened in the firelight and seemed to reflect their own color upon the face of the girl.

'I am not hungry,' she said.

He saw that her eyes were downward, upon the fire, and an unreasonable anger came upon Thunder Moon. He seized the whip which lay beside him and with it struck the ground.

'Eat!' he commanded.

Without a word, she reached for a morsel of the meat and obeyed him. He forgot his own food and leaned forward to watch, for this simple action of hers filled him with a strange satisfaction. Only one thing was needed to make his pleasure perfect, and that was that he should have slain the game with his own hands.

Twice she stopped, and twice with a gesture he forced her to continue.

'Is that meat poison, Red Wind?' he asked her at length.

Instead of answering, she merely lifted her head and looked steadfastly at him, and he stared in return, looking deeply into her eyes. Even by firelight, the intense, rich blue of them was apparent to him, like water under a deep sky.

'Tell me, Red Wind,' he asked again, 'why is it that you speak to other men and tell them lies about me?'

He was tremendously irritated when she refused to answer him, merely continuing her grave observance of his face.

'Why is it,' he went on, 'that you stole out with the Pawnee wolf, Rising Cloud, and told him such a lie as this, that I am not an Indian at all, but a white man? How could you find such a lie in your heart?'

'Is it a lie?' she asked him in her quiet voice.

The simple question shocked all the blood from his heart to his head and made his face burn. 'Am I like one of those cringing, sneaking people?' he asked. 'Am I like a mangy coyote which dares not eat until after the wolf has left the prey?'

'Are the white men like that?' she returned.

'Are they not? What do they have except what the red people leave for them on the plains? How do they live except by the wealth of the Cheyennes and the others who ride on the plains?'

She waited a moment and then, as though she forced herself to speak, she said slowly: 'I have been to two trading forts. I have talked with trappers and with soldiers. Some of them are bad men, but all of them are wise. They told me of great cities beyond the Father of Waters. They told me of cities so great that into one of them could be poured all of the tribes of the red men who ride on the plains.'

'Do you believe such lies?' he asked her scornfully.

She went on, after another little pause. 'They are so rich that in one of their cities are more wonderful things than all the prairies and all the thousands of thousands of buffalo. They build canoes in which five hundred men sit, and those canoes are driven by fire, fast as a horse can run on the firm land, and also over the land, they send wagons of fire that. . . .'

'Red Wind,' said the warrior, 'I listen to you and I wish not to smile. I see that they have told you such lies as even children, among the Suhtai, would laugh at.'

'I also laughed,' said the girl, 'but then I went to the edge of the great river with my father and up the stream. Through the night we saw lights coming, and there was a great roaring like many winds although the winds were still, and up the waters against the current where no Indian could drive a canoe a monstrous boat came. It had many bright eyes that threw rays of light across the prairie. Above its head rushed and roared a great hand of flame that drew down and leaped up again. All over the boat we saw people walking.'

Thunder Moon moistened his dry lips with the tip of his tongue. He lighted his pipe and first blew a breath toward the sky and then a breath toward the ground. After that he crouched on his heels and smoked slowly, contemplatively. Wild thoughts were passing through his mind.

'I have heard you,' he said at last. 'I do not wish to believe that you say a thing that is not. But if they have such magic as this, why do not the white men drive the Indians from the prairie?'

'It is not magic. Medicine men do not make the fire-boats. Medicine men do nothing among the white men. Only they talk a great deal. They do nothing else. With their hands, the white men make these things. When they wish to take the prairies from us, then they will take them. An old man among the Omissis has told me so. I have seen the boat of fire. And I believe.'

'This is very well,' said Thunder Moon. 'No matter what the old man may have told you, we are still plainly the chosen people of Tarawa and never may be destroyed by the white men. Perhaps you did not altogether despise me when you said that I was a white man?'

She would not answer again, leaving that very open opportunity for giving him a handsome compliment.

'At least,' said Thunder Moon, 'tell me for what reason you called me a white man?'

'Can we tell a dog from a wolf?' she asked him in return.

'Surely we can do that.'

'By what tokens?' asked the girl.

'The wolf has a looser skin. He has stronger jaws. He is more wise on the trail. He is more quick to flee and he is more terrible to fight.'

'If you see a dog with a loose skin, with powerful jaws, wise on the trail, quick to flee, but terrible in fight?'

'That would be no dog, but a wolf.'

'True,' said the girl. 'So I see you, Thunder Moon, and I call you a white man because you and all of your ways are white.'

He listened like a man bereft of his wits. 'Is this the truth that you speak and not a thing to merely anger me?' he asked her.

'You too are a great warrior,' she said, 'and so are the white men, though you do not believe it. They count no coups and take no scalps. Neither does Thunder Moon. You make no medicine. Neither do the white men. The white men make their squaws into men and their men into squaws. And so do you.'

She did not alter her voice as she delivered the last stinging sentence. Therefore it was a moment before Thunder Moon understood her meaning and he turned a deep crimson, a furious, deep crimson.

'It is time to mount,' he said hoarsely, and he started to his feet.

# 24

# Some Other Differences

He knew, even as he climbed into the saddle, that he had not even then taken the true Cheyenne course with her. For most of the stalwart braves would have rewarded this final speech of Red Wind's by throwing a handful of dust into her face and then flogging her soundly. However, all he could do as Standing Antelope put out the fire was to ride up to her and say grimly: 'You speak evil of the whites. Are your own eyes and your own hair black?'

The last ray from the fire illumined her face. It was utterly blank and the expression indecipherable. Yes, no matter what the color of skin, hair, and eyes, her heart was the heart of a true Cheyenne. He knew it, and her silence laid a load upon his heart. He wanted an answer, but she gave him no opportunity with her muteness.

So they journeyed on through the darkness. It was a double night to Thunder Moon. They entered the village and instantly their coming was known. Boys and women flocked out from the teepees and rushed around Red Wind, screaming at her and calling her vile names. For she had committed the last crime for a Cheyenne girl – she had fled with one of their most detested enemies. One woman leaped up and caught Red Wind by the sleeve to drag her from the back of her pony. Once pulled down into the midst of those reaching hands, she would be scratched, beaten, torn, and disfigured for all her life. Thunder Moon waited for her scream for help.

No scream came. She struck away the hands that gripped her. Three or four more vengeful squaws grappled with her, and Thunder Moon had to ride in among them and brush them away. They fell back before him, calling him a fool, begging him to let them work their revenge upon this traitor to her nation. He promised them his whip across their faces if they rushed at the girl again.

So they rode through the camp and, when they were close to the lodge of Big Hard Face, they passed the teepee of Three Bears. That hero stood before the open flap of his home, illumined faintly by the firelight which flickered within. No doubt his heart was bursting with curiosity to learn all that had happened on this trail, but he remained with folded arms, immobile.

Thunder Moon drew rein and he grimly noted that the girl, even if she were unwilling to appeal to him in the midst of danger, at least dared not to ride on without his protection. She turned her horse beside him.

'Three Bears,' said the warrior, 'I took your boy away with me. He had no name and the braves did not know him. I bring him back a man.'

There was a stifled cry from the squaw of Three Bears and a deep shout from the excited listeners who had pressed around, but Three Bears did not stir.

'The quickest eye and the truest ear belongs to him,' went on Thunder Moon. 'Therefore his name is Standing Antelope. The Pawnee was wily and cunning, but Standing Antelope was wiser by far. The Pawnee rode fast and well, but Standing Antelope rode faster. The Pawnee turned to fight for his life. His spear was in his hand. Standing Antelope rushed in and counted his coup.'

A wild uproar of applause followed this statement. Then silence followed to hear the result of the fight.

'Why should we kill a wounded wolf? We sent Rising Cloud on to his people to let them know that before long we should come again and strike them, and leave the plains covered with their dead men and send their ghosts to die in the wind.

'We come back to you. If any man doubts that Standing Antelope is a warrior, let him look and see that he carries a spear and a rifle and a revolver that speaks six words. With every one, a man may die.'

The boy could endure the strain no longer but, flinging himself from his horse, he fell into the arms of his father. His mother clutched him then. Hubbub broke loose around them. Thunder Moon turned away with the girl toward his own tent. As he went, he could hear behind him a shrill, boyish voice chanting over the tumult, chanting the first of his war songs, telling how he, Standing Antelope, won the name of a warrior and counted his first coup upon the body of a Pawnee chief.

It gave Thunder Moon a certain solace in the midst of the darkness which was settling over his mind. He dismounted and waved the girl before him into the lodge where White Crow and Big Hard Face waited for them. The noise had apprised them of what to expect, and the tongue of the hag was well loosened for her work. She sprang up and hurled a torrent of insults at the head of the girl. Red Wind, her hands clasped loosely before her, endured the storm without a rejoinder.

'Stop her tongue,' said Thunder Moon to his foster father.

'Be still,' commanded Big Hard Face.

'It is only the beginning of her evil!' exclaimed the squaw. 'Walking Horse gave us the price of fifty horses for keeping her. But she will do us harm to the value of a thousand horses before the wicked spirits come for her, like brothers for a sister.'

Big Hard Face raised his hand and White Crow relapsed into an angry mumbling.

Thunder Moon beckoned and Big Hard Face came out with him into the open night. They walked together without a word through the village, taking care to avoid all who were abroad. That was not difficult. Behind them the first war song of Standing Antelope was gathering a crowd and there the boys, mad with envy, went to hear him. There the warriors gathered to encourage such deeds of valor in the youth of the tribe.

Out upon the prairie went the two and reached the bank of the river and sat on a fallen log. Beneath them, the stream ran black and smooth, with the faces of the stars fallen in it like flecks of cold fire.

'What about Rising Cloud?' asked Big Hard Face at last, as though they had discussed all other things except the fate of the Pawnee warrior.

'He was sent to his own people freely,' said Thunder Moon. 'I could not kill a helpless man.'

Big Hard Face stifled an exclamation. 'That mercy will cost many a Cheyenne scalp,' he said. 'Do you think that there is gratitude or kindness among the Pawnee wolves?'

'I think nothing,' said Thunder Moon. 'I am very sick.' Stretching his arms around his foster father, he bowed his head on the shoulder of that venerable chief. Who else of all the brave among the Suhtai would have been guilty of such weakness? But the heart of Big Hard Face swelled in him with pain and sorrow.

'All that is evil comes from woman,' said Big Hard Face. 'But all the harm that an old wise woman can do is nothing compared with the danger that lies in a beautiful girl. I shall tell you why Walking Horse sent her away instead of marrying her to a man among the Omissis. He is the foremost of all of their chiefs. His war raids have taken him from the Sioux to the Comanches. When he was in the southland, he took from the Comanches a woman they had captured in Mexico. He made her his squaw and, before she died, she gave him this daughter. When she grew older, every young man among the Omissis coveted her. They tied their horses at the lodge door of Walking Horse. They tied ten, twenty, thirty horses at the lodge post. But still the girl would not have any of them for a husband.

'Walking Horse feared to give her away because, if he married her to one warrior, she might smile on another and that would mean war in the camp. The braves began to hate Walking Horse because they thought that he would not give the girl to them. Once a bullet sang past his head as he walked through his own camp. Twice knives were drawn against him. Then he saw what he must do. He came to the Suhtai and settled amongst us until he discovered the lodge where the strongest man dwelt. To that lodge he gave the girl. Being an honest man, he gave a great prize with her. Now I shall gather together the prize which he paid down with her and take her and the treasure back to him.'

'No,' said Thunder Moon.

His foster father was silent, grimly filled with thought.

'She has found the way into your heart,' he said. 'But do not take her for your squaw. She has soft hands. She will not make your lodge happy or fill it with robes which she has dressed. There is no labor in her. Not words but work makes a good wife. I shall tell you about women. They have long hair but little wisdom. They are a trouble when they are with us, but we miss them when they are away. Only to make mischief they are wiser than men. If they obey, it is because they wish to rule. It is easy for them to laugh and easier for them to weep.

'Men paint their faces to be terrible to their enemies; women paint their faces to betray their friends. It is dangerous to be loved by them. It is worse to be hated by them. She speaks best when she thinks least, for in all things she is the opposite of men and she wants too much of all things. She is beautiful, but she is soon old. She always has words but she seldom has meaning. Where she is, there is sure to be noise. She is more filled with cunning than a coyote and, though you watch her, you cannot keep her from stealing from you. A man may lie gravely, but a woman lies with a smile. Moreover, a man repents, but a woman never sees her own faults. Her only knowledge is that she is right. When she smiles, soon you will have to spend treasure. If she loves finery, only the entrance to the lodge will be kept in order. If she loves talk, her husband never shall sleep. Whether she laughs, or cries, or sings, no man can understand her true meaning. We think that we possess her; it is she who possesses us. Though she is mysterious, she is a great fool, for she loves words more than deeds, and a boaster more than a modest man.

'Tell her that she is lovely and she soon is a greater fool than ever. So from these things, my son, you will see that it is much better to live without a wife. Or if you have a woman in your lodge, let her be an old drudge and not really your squaw. If you let a woman bear a child to you, then she never will have done until she has made you her slave. She does not live to know herself, but to make others believe great things about her. She would rather be beautiful than good or wise. Therefore tell me, my son, that if this woman has stolen into your heart, you will put her out again straightway.'

'Father,' said Thunder Moon, 'she hates me with all her heart, but I never shall be happy until she is my squaw.'

# 25

# To His Own People

If Big Hard Face was half troglodyte, he also was half philosopher. He listened to the words of his foster son with interest but without speaking for some time. Finally he said gravely: 'When a man desires a thing greatly, there is a time when it is best to study not whether the thing is good or bad, but how it can be gotten. Now you wish to know whether or not you can win the love of this woman?'

'No,' said Thunder Moon, raising his head, 'for first of all I wish to ask you about the things which she has said to me. You, Big Hard Face, are my father.'

'It is true,' answered the Cheyenne.

'Then how,' said Thunder Moon, 'can I be called a white man?'

Big Hard Face started violently. Then, turning to Thunder Moon, he asked sharply: 'She has put that question in your mind?'

'What does it matter?' replied the warrior. 'The question is asked.'

'It is the Omissis girl,' said the chief savagely. 'Who knows a child so well as the parent? If I had guessed that such an evil spirit were in the girl, I never should have taken the price of the fifty horses from her father when he came to us and begged us to take his daughter into our lodge.'

'This is a simple thing,' replied Thunder Moon. 'I have asked you a question and all that is needed is for you to answer: "No! There is no drop of the false blood of a white man in your veins." '

The chief considered for a moment. 'I have taught you that the white men are partly villains and partly fools, have I not?' he asked.

'You have taught me that,' replied Thunder Moon. 'But between me and the other braves of the Suhtai I feel that there is a difference, and Red Wind says that it is the difference between the red man and the white. Where the moccasin covers my feet, the skin is white.'

'It is better,' said Big Hard Face, 'to consider the chattering of prairie dogs at the entrance to their holes than to worry about the words of woman. We have talked enough, my son. Let us go home to the lodge and sleep.'

The mightiest hand among all the Cheyennes was laid upon the shoulder of Big Hard Face. 'Wait a little,' said Thunder Moon.

The chief listened, leaning forward a little.

'You are sad,' said Thunder Moon. 'Why is that?'

'I am sad because when I was a young brave, the warriors did not listen to the lying voices of the women.' He nodded his head as though considering again the faults of these unregenerate days, or reading again some postil in the margin of his vision.

'The color of my skin says that the woman is right,' replied Thunder Moon.

'It is because you wish it,' answered the chief. 'You wish to be one of these strange people. You wish to call yourself white, and to leave your people and go among the strangers.'

'Look,' said Thunder Moon. He pointed. The moon was rising, and in the direction of its broad and golden horn he extended his arm.

'I see it,' replied the chief.

'Would not a man be a fool to give his word in the presence of the Sky People when he wished to speak a lie?'

Big Hard Face was silent.

'Yet I promise you,' said the warrior, 'that it is not so much what the woman has said as it is something inside my heart that makes me ask you these questions. Open your heart to me. Admit it once that I am not like the rest of the Suhtai. Where they smile, I am sad. Where they are sad, I smile. Who is there among the Suhtai that does not shudder when Spotted Bull frowns? But I have no fear of his medicine. I have seen you tremble before him, even my father, even Big Hard Face. But I laugh at Spotted Bull and his foolish talk. He cannot make the sky either pale or blue for all of his medicine. Also the ways of the Cheyenne upon the war path are not my ways. The coups and the scalps which they prize are not my prizes. In everything we are different.'

'Look at the horse herd,' answered the chief with much warmth. 'Though the dame and the sire are the same, what two colts are alike? One is a fool and a sluggard and the other is as swift as the wind.'

'That is true. But men are not like horses. I run swifter but not so far as the Cheyennes. I am stronger in my hands. With a gun I am more sure. I cannot endure pain as they endure it. Every moment that I draw my breath I know that I am not like my brothers of the Suhtai.'

'It is the woman who talks by your lips,' answered Big Hard Face, grown sullen.

'It is not the woman. What other brave has killed as I have killed? When I ride out to the battle, the Pawnees divide before me. The Comanches scream to one another. Ten men ride against me, but even all the ten shrink before they come close. The Sioux know me and the Blackfoot run before my face. The Crows cry in their lodges for the dead men who have fallen before me. What other Suhtai has killed as I have killed or been such a power in battle? Or in the council, who makes the old men grow silent when he speaks? To whom do the old men listen? It is to me! Still, I am not a chief. The young warriors say: "He never endured the trial of pain. When his father would have pierced his breasts and tied the thongs in the flesh, he screamed and refused the test. His shame is before our eyes." Therefore, Big Hard Face, it is plain that I am not like the others. Red Wind says that it is because I am a white man. You must tell me the truth, for I see that you are not speaking with all your mind to me.'

Big Hard Face started to his feet. 'I shall go back to my lodge,' he said, 'and take the woman and give her the whip across her shoulders. I shall make her admit before your face that she says the thing which is not true!'

'Do not touch her,' said Thunder Moon. 'You are no longer young. There is little power in your hands. Do not touch her!'

'Because you would fight me for her sake?' exclaimed the chief.

'I have not said it.'

'I hear it in your voice.'

'Perhaps it is true.'

Big Hard Face flung his robe over his head. 'My own son raises his hand against me,' he said. 'It is time for me to go out in the winter and let the wolves gather around me. I no longer am valued in my own lodge, and my son lifts his hand against me.'

He turned away toward the village, but the great form of Thunder Moon strode before him.

'I have asked you many questions,' he said. 'The man who does not wish to answer finds many chances to fall into anger. If you leave me now, I shall believe all that Red Wind has told me.'

Big Hard Face recoiled from him. 'Then what would you do?' he asked.

'Blood calls out to the heart of a man,' said Thunder Moon. 'I should go to my people and learn the ways of their speech.'

'Go, go!' cried Big Hard Face. 'Go, and let us remain behind you with an empty lodge! For this I have raised you! For this I have been a father to you! Would your own mother have labored for you as White Crow has worked? Would your own father have given you such horses and such weapons?' He checked himself as his tongue was about to run on, but already he had said far too much.

'Then it is true!' cried Thunder Moon in a broken voice. 'All that Red Wind said is true and I am not a son of the Cheyennes. Far off in a lodge of the white men, my father and my true mother mourn for me. In the winter they are hungry because I am not there to hunt for them. In the summer, the white braves scorn them because they are poor and have to walk beside the dogs which drag their travois.'

'No, no!' exclaimed Big Hard Face, waxing warm. 'You speak like a fool. The home in which your father and mother live is greater than fifty lodges such as mine. Black-faced Negroes work for them. In their lands many fine horses are grazing. They are rich. All the wealth of the Suhtai is hardly equal to the wealth of your father and your mother.'

Thunder Moon was silent. In the silence Big Hard Face came to realize that he had, indeed, spoken far too much. He gathered the robe closer about his head and started back toward the lights of the village, but his foster son did not follow him. Suddenly he returned to Thunder Moon and dropped his robe to the ground. The moon played upon his old body, heavy but still strong.

'Oh, Thunder Moon,' he said, 'what is it that you do? Do you renounce the Suhtai who have been your brothers? Do you give them up for a strange people? What is the color of the skin? It is the color of the heart that matters!'

'I am a Suhtai,' said Thunder Moon gravely. 'I am a Suhtai and nothing shall make me have another self. I am a Suhtai, but now I see that I am a Suhtai only in my love and my thoughts. In every other thing, I am a white man and among the white men I belong. Like them, I must learn to live as a coyote lives, eating the carrion which the wolves leave after their feasts on the buffalo which they have pulled down.'

Big Hard Face reached out his hands and found those of his son. He gripped them hard. 'Now I part from myself the thing which I have loved more than I have loved life!' he said. 'I part myself from what is best and dearest to me in the world. But out of wrong no right can grow, and I have done wrong, and therefore I must be punished. The Sky People whom I thought loved me have treated me as a fool is treated. They have let me grow old before they showed that they hate me. Sit down, and I shall tell you everything as it came to pass.'

'You are tired and sick at heart,' said Thunder Moon, trembling with excitement. 'Wait until tomorrow. Then we shall talk again about these matters.'

'There is no tomorrow for me,' answered Big Hard Face sadly. 'What life has a childless man? Now I am childless! The women scream and cut their flesh for the sake of their dead sons. But I cannot scream and gash myself. For I have no son. All these days I have lived a lie. My teepee has been empty even when I let Thunder Moon fill it with honor and with fame. I have no son and the son I had was only a sham and a pretense.'

# 26

# An Old, Unhappy Man

'What is an old man but an unhappy man?' said the chief to his foster son. 'Age makes a man gray, but it does not make him happy. It is a sad guest in the lodge. Old age is like a smoking fire. Even though the greatest chief lives to the greatest age, still he must die at last. Is not this true?'

'Perhaps it is true,' said Thunder Moon, taking pity on the manifest grief of his foster father.

'What is the cure, then, for age?' asked the chief.

'I cannot tell.'

'Think, however.'

'I cannot tell, for the same cure would be a cure for death also.'

'There is a cure for death, oh, Thunder Moon!'

'Then I cannot guess it, for the stoutest of the buffalo will grow old and die at last.'

'Then I shall tell you. A father lives after death in his son. For when death puts an end to the swiftest and the longest race, still something may be left after. The bow may be grasped by another hand. The horse may be bestrode by another warrior. The lodge may shelter another, and the Tarawa to whom the father prayed will send fortune to the heir. It is in our children that we live again. And the hope of our children makes death a shadow which otherwise could be a terrible force and steal every moment of happiness from our lips. So I tell you these things because, as I speak to you, so it was with me. I was a great warrior. I had many horses. No lodge was greater than mine. In no teepee was there more meat. All the wise men in the tribe listened when I spoke at the council. But as the time grew, I still had no squaw. Do you ask me why, Thunder Moon?'

The foster son held silence.

'Because my face is cursed with ugliness,' said Big Hard Face. 'The women would not look at me. They turned away their faces when I was near them and, when I had gone by, I could hear them laughing. So I could not take a squaw who would give me a child. As for women for their own sake, I never prized them. We cannot live except through another, but mothers are loved by their children only.

'So I grew older, and I looked around me and saw that a time would come when I should have great wealth, but there would be in my lodge no young man growing wise and strong to take in his hands the weapons which some day I should have to lay down. There would be no one to sit by me when I was ill, and there would be no one to catch my horse and saddle it when I grew weak. The more I thought of these things, the sicker and the feebler of heart I became.

'At last I saw that I could have no happiness unless I did something to cure this evil. So I thought long and hard on that matter and at last I determined on the thing to do. He who wants the fastest horse in the world cannot expect to find it in the next lodge and, if he does, another warrior says that it is his. So I decided that for the thing that I wanted I should ride to a great distance and try to find between the east and the west something which would be worth giving up my life, and some great action by which the Cheyenne nation might remember me even if I grew old without an heir.

'So I crossed the dark of that night and the whiteness of the day many times. I came to rivers and followed some along the banks, and others I swam across with my horse, but still I came to nothing which seemed worth dying for. At last, I came to the land of the white men.'

Here Big Hard Face paused. Though Thunder Moon now could guess what was coming, he said not a word.

'I journeyed a great distance among the lodges of the white men. They had teepees built of stone and of wood and there were grass lands and fruit lands. There were many horses and cattle, and such richness that nothing in the world could have been worth it except the open freedom of the prairies. Never had I seen such things, and never have I dared to speak of them among the Suhtai for fear that men would laugh at me.'

'What things, then, did you see?' asked Thunder Moon hoarsely.

'The trails that they traveled were made of rock broken and laid thick upon the ground. Ten thousand buffalo might run across them in the rainy season and never break their surface into mud.'

There was a grunt of wonder from the warrior.

'The smallest lodge that I looked at was so large that two or three of the finest teepees among the Suhtai could be put in it. All around their houses in the fields grow all the fruits and the corn that men could want for eating. They do not ride on the war path. They may sit still at home and there they will have all that they wish. There is more wealth for one of those great lodges than for all the Suhtai nation.'

'Then it is true!' said Thunder Moon in amazement, 'for now two tongues have said it.'

'At last,' said the chief, 'I came to a place of many great trees and I rode through fields, and there were no houses for a great distance. I came to the greatest house that I had ever seen. It was so great that I trembled when I saw it. Some came from several places at its top. I thought surely that Tarawa must live there. I lay in the woods, moving slowly from place to place that day, watching the great house and wondering. Everywhere I saw Negroes working in the fields, or coming back from the fields to little lodges built not far from the great one. Then I came to a pasture and in that pasture I saw the finest horses in the whole world. I took some of them. You know about them. They are the chestnuts whom you yourself have ridden against every one of our enemies, and they never have failed you in battle or flight or hunting. I saw them standing in the field together, and I trembled again. "These are the horses on whose backs Tarawa dashes across the skies," I said to myself.

'But they were very gentle. When I came to them, they let me take them. They were like colts, too young to know what fear is. I took some of them and especially I took the great stallion, the king of the band.

'Then I lay in the woods close to the house, waiting for the night to come before I started away. As I lay there, I saw a Negro woman come out from the house carrying with her a small white child and she put the child under a tree.

'I crept a little closer. I looked at that child. I thought that I would take a scalp and go back to the Cheyennes with a white scalp and the great horses. So when the woman went away, I went to the infant. It was not afraid, Thunder Moon. It lifted up its hands to me. I could not help picking it up and carrying it away with me. I said that the Sky People knew that I wanted fast horses and a son, and they had led me where I could find both. I carried the child away. I was hunted for many days by the white men. But at last I came to the open country, and then nothing could keep me from winning that race, for the chestnuts were working under me. That is the story, Thunder Moon. You know how you have grown up in my teepee. My blood is not your blood. My thoughts are not your thoughts. I am Suhtai and you are not. But a place is in my heart for you. Tell me if there is a place in yours for me?'

'Hear me, Sky People!' cried Thunder Moon enthusiastically. 'I know that you brought me onto the plains so that I could live with your chosen race. As for my real father and mother, they were nothing to me. I only know the lodge of Big Hard Face. Therefore I never. . . .'

'Speak slowly!' said the wise old brave. 'There is nothing so easily broken as a promise which a man does not want to keep. If you have not seen your father and your mother, nevertheless they have seen you. If you have forgotten them, they have not forgotten you.'

'What do you mean?' asked Thunder Moon, much disturbed.

'Tarawa has heed of the white man and the black, as well as of the red,' declared the old chief. 'So he has knowledge of you here and, of course, he has had knowledge of the sorrow of your father and your mother.'

Thunder Moon fell into a great trouble, but at last he said hurriedly: 'I shall tell you. If they have not forgotten me, then they are dead. I do not feel them calling to my heart.'

'You will hear them afterward,' said the chief. 'Now you are too full of trouble because of the woman. Because of her, you will have more troubles still. Now let us go home, Thunder Moon. Still for a little time my lodge is your lodge, and my home is your home. Afterward, you will begin to turn to your own people. Ah, and I have been like a fool. If one clips the wing of an eagle, still the feathers will grow again.'

To this Thunder Moon began an emotional protest that he never would leave the lodge of his foster father, and that to the end of his life he would be true to him and remain.

Big Hard Face cut him short, saying bluntly: 'I am old, and old men love to talk much, but not to listen.'

So they walked on in silence, and Big Hard Face went slower and slower till it seemed as though he were changing his mind with every step that he made.

'Go slowly, go slowly,' said the chief. 'I am not a boy. I am not a young buck. I am very old.'

When they came to the edge of the camp, Big Hard Face declared that he wished to walk to see a friend, and he added bitterly to his foster son: 'Besides, you'll want to go off by yourself and think of this thing . . . and how you came from strange people . . . and how quickly you can go to see their faces. At least, you will want to run to see the woman.'

Big Hard Face walked off alone and Thunder Moon went quietly back toward his teepee, his head raised so high that the lights of the stars twisted and swirled and dazzled in his eyes, and wild new thoughts and fears and hopes began to storm through his brain.

He might have walked in this fashion, straight into the hands of death. Only the glint of the danger he saw with the corner of his eyes and leaped aside and whirled in time to meet the lunging shadow and the knife which was its darting point. He grappled with the brave who held the weapon and, then with an exclamation of horror, he sprang back from the murderer. He recognized Snake-That-Talks, one of his oldest and closest friends in the tribe.

# 27

# In the Firelit Teepee

The other did not attempt to skulk away. For a moment he poised the knife flat in the palm of his hand, as though ready to hurl it at Thunder Moon, but then – perhaps realizing that this was a weak defense against the 'medicine' which hung in the holster beside the other's thigh – he dropped the weapon back into its sheath and folded his arms. There was no finer presence among all the tall ranks of the Suhtai than Snake-That-Talks, and even by starlight he made an imposing figure.

'Brother,' said Thunder Moon sadly, 'we have been friends for many years. With you I went on the war trail when we entered the land of the Comanches and took away their great medicine, The Yellow Man. Your lodge has been open to me and my lodge has been open to you. In the winter famines we have given meat to one another. Of the last pemmican in your lodge, I have taken half. But now you have come to kill me. How have I wronged you, brother? What do I own that should be yours?'

The Suhtai seemed unable to answer for a moment but then he said slowly: 'The woman in your teepee smiled at me. That is all.'

'It is Red Wind again,' groaned Thunder Moon. 'She is not a woman but an evil spirit! Oh, Snake-That-Talks, you already have a squaw and two children in your lodge.'

To this the Indian made no answer, and Thunder Moon turned

away and stumbled on toward his home. For Red Wind he kept a strange fury in his mind, for he knew that she had stolen away one of his nearest friends with a single glance. He had spared the life of the young brave. For that very reason, Snake-That-Talks never could forgive him.

When he came closer to his teepee, he was aware of a number of young men loitering here and there and he passed slowly among them, expecting that they had been driven there by a wish to speak with him – perhaps to propose some feat of war. However, not one of them paid any attention to him, but allowed him to go past them while they continued to stroll in an apparently aimless manner. What could have brought them here, Thunder Moon could not guess, unless indeed it were the singing of a girl within the teepee of his foster father. A rich, low-pitched, rather husky voice was chanting a song which went straight to the ears of Thunder Moon, and he understood instantly why the loiterers were gathered in front of his lodge. It was Red Wind's song which had brought them, as surely as summer skies bring the birds. It was Red Wind's song also which made these youthful warriors oblivious to his coming. All at once his passions mastered him and carried him away, like a boat sloping down a lee tide. He felt that this girl who sat in his teepee was bringing about him dangers which, sooner or later, must overwhelm him.

He strode into the entrance of the lodge. The moment he appeared the song stopped, as though he had struck the singer. Yonder sat Red Wind, staring down to the ground in all humility. Or was it humility, indeed? Suddenly he felt more hate than kindness for her – hatred and fear mixed together, for he wanted to catch her by the arm and drag her to a place where the firelight would shine upon her guilty face, but he dared not touch her.

'Red Wind!' he said.

She lifted her head obediently and looked toward him. But she might as well have continued to stare at the ground, so dense was the veil which she had dropped across her eyes.

'I have met Snake-That-Talks,' he said, and waited to see the flickering shadow of guilt across her face.

No shadow touched it. She was like one who sleeps with open eyes.

White Crow slipped nearer, her eyes hungry with mischief, as though she guessed that trouble was about to descend upon the head of the young woman, and as though she reveled in the prospect.

'Go out from the teepee!' Thunder Moon commanded her.

'It is come to this,' whined White Crow. 'I am driven out from the lodge which I made with my own hands. Who else cleaned all those buffalo hides? Who prepared them? Who set up this teepee, so that it looked like a pyramid of snow in the spring? Now you are driving me away to shiver in the cold and. . . .'

A wave of Thunder Moon's arm convinced her that she would have to obey. She shuffled through the entrance and disappeared.

'Now,' said Thunder Moon to the girl, 'let me know what it is that you want?'

She looked up at him, her eyes still vague, though a meaning was beginning to come into them.

'Snake-That-Talks is a great warrior,' said Thunder Moon in continuation. 'There is hardly a braver or a keener man among the Suhtai. You showed that you are clever and wise when you picked him out and sent him to murder me.'

She closed her eyes. 'Murder?' breathed the girl.

He strode fiercely to understand what was in her voice – horror, or disappointment, or perhaps merely fear of the punishment which now might hang over her head.

'You sent him,' said the warrior. 'You put the knife in his hand and you sent him out to find me and to kill me. Then you would go to his lodge and be his squaw.'

With a curious detachment, she looked up to him as he stood in the firelight, a mastodontic form with his shadow floating on the white teepee wall behind him. Light-footed, massive of shoulder, proud of head, if ever a man walked who seemed typical of all that an Indian warrior should be, such seemed the foster son of Big Hard Face on this very night when he had learned that he was not an Indian at all.

'Confess it!' he said, grown more savage during her silence. For a strange fear was entering him. At one moment she seemed to him the only reality he ever had looked upon. Again she seemed a very Maya of beautiful illusion. 'But you know that he had tried and failed. Some shadowy owl or bat flew into your lodge and sat on your shoulder, so that the old eyes of White Crow could not see it. It told you everything that had happened.'

Such stories he had used for his mirth in another day, but now he looked upon her seriously as an occultist, for how else to define her he knew not.

She said quietly: 'Do you believe in talking birds?'

'I believe in evil spirits, and I know that there is one in you,' he cried. 'No other woman could do as you have done. There is nothing but danger and harm in you. To your father you showed that. Now you show it to me. I cannot tell why I do not tie you hand and foot and set you out on the prairie where the wolves might eat you.'

She said, rather in curiosity than in fear he thought: 'The promise you gave to my father keeps you from doing that.'

'When you put a knife in the hand of Snake-That-Talks,' replied Thunder Moon, 'you set me free from that oath.'

'Here is the only knife that I own,' she said. 'Was it this knife that Snake-That-Talks used against you?'

'You looked at him,' replied Thunder Moon, 'and the evil spirit in you possessed him! Now you have called other young men of the Suhtai together. They stand in front of my lodge and listen to your voice and every one of them has a knife ready against me. Why do you do these things, Red Wind? How have I harmed you? When have I laid a heavy hand upon you? Have I forced you to become my squaw against your will? Have I forced you to do more work? Have I forced you to carry heavy weights, or to flesh the hides, or to tire your eyes and your quick fingers putting beads upon moccasins? In what way have I wronged you or been cruel to you?'

The heart of the warrior swelled in him as he spoke. In all the seasons of his life, nothing had stirred him so much as this interview with the maiden of the Omissis.

'You have not wronged me,' said the girl. 'It is my father who has wronged me.'

He breathed more freely. But he added: 'Then what can I do to make you happy? What can I do to keep you from arming my best friends against me?'

'When I first came to you,' said the girl, in her quiet voice, 'you could have taken the price of the fifty horses and given it back to my father, and given me back to him along with it.'

'Do you wish me to do that?' he asked her.

'I wished it then,' she said. 'I think that I wished it then. But now it is too late. Now I think that it is much too late.'

'Why is it too late, Red Wind?'

'If you think about it a little quietly, then you would know why.'

He grew wildly angry again. Once, as he had ridden the plains, he had seen a hawk strike a small bird in mid-air and lighting on a stunted tree hackle it with talons and beak. He was moved to throw himself on this strange creature now and destroy her because of the mystery which she opposed against him at all times.

'Am I a child without wits?' he asked the girl. 'Have I not thought about this thing until my brain aches?'

'Yes,' she agreed, unheedful of his passion, 'I suppose that thinking may not help, after all. Either one knows or one does not know.'

'I shall do it!' exclaimed Thunder Moon. 'I shall gather together all the treasure that your father gave to us. If it were ten times as great, it would not be enough to make up for the pain I suffer in keeping you. I shall gather everything together and more, and take you with the price back to the Omissis.'

'When will you do it?' she asked.

'I? Tomorrow!'

She smiled, faintly.

'Why do you smile, Red Wind? You make me very angry when you act as though you knew things which I cannot know.'

She wove her fingers into one massive braid of her hair and watched him. 'I think it is too late for me and for you,' she said sadly. 'I don't think that you will give back the price to my father or give me back with it. There is nothing but trouble before us.'

He was about to speak again when Big Hard Face entered the teepee, and the conversation was broken off short.

# 28

# A Wicked Witch

White Crow entered almost right behind her nephew. The ancient woman was trembling with malice. 'This wicked witch,' she cried to Big Hard Face, 'has been sitting here singing love songs and gathering the young men around the lodge.'

'Wait,' broke in Thunder Moon. 'They were not love songs. I heard her singing.'

'Whatever she sings is a love song!' exclaimed White Crow. 'The young men came and walked before this teepee. You drove me out as if I were a dog. And the young men came to me one by one. "Is all well with Red Wind?" they asked. They could hear you talking loudly to her, and they frowned when they heard the loudness of your voice. Do you see what the curse is that she has brought to this lodge, Big Hard Face?'

That chief, however, had retired to the darkness which surrounded his couch and there he sat, almost lost to view. White Crow peered at him, opened her withered lips to say something more, and then peered more closely and discovered that even the dimness of that place was not sufficiently dark for Big Hard Face. He had covered his head with his robe, like one who mourns. At that her malice seemed to grow in her. She hurried closer. In her dangling arms, there seemed as much lean, sinewy strength as ever, but her back was bent with years.

'Son,' she said to the old chief, 'what is the sorrow that has fallen on you?'

He did not answer.

Then she screamed at him, shaking her bony fists: 'I am not a woman! I am dirt! I am nothing! I only live to work till I die. No one will listen to me. No heart is open to me. In my own lodge, that I made with my own hands, I am nothing. But I shall not endure it. The river will take my body. Or I can go to the lodge of a friend. . . .'

'Be quiet,' said Thunder Moon angrily. 'All the ears in every teepee near us will hear you.'

'Let them hear me!' shrieked the squaw. 'I shall go now and sing my song in front of the lodge and let them know how I live here.'

The deep, heavy, lifeless voice of the chief spoke to her: 'Woman, woman, make no more noise. Or else sit in the ashes and weep, but not for yourself.'

At this solemn speech, White Crow clung to the post from which the medicine bag and the weapons of Big Hard Face hung.

'What has happened?' she whispered.

'We are alone,' said Big Hard Face.

'We are not alone,' said the squaw, mistaking his meaning. 'The evil woman from the Omissis is here with us, and Thunder Moon who thinks I am only a dog.'

'We are alone,' said the chief, more heavily than before. 'Thunder Moon is gone. He is drawn away to his own people.'

'What are his people?' gasped the squaw. 'Are they not our people? Are you not his father? Does he not belong to the Suhtai, sing their songs, fight their battles? Big Hard Face, do not talk like a fool.'

'He is gone to his own people,' answered the chief again. 'The Omissis girl opened his eyes. She showed him the truth. Soon we shall lose him. Now, let me be in peace.' He drew the robe slowly over his head again.

White Crow, as though suddenly gone blind, reached about until she found Thunder Moon, and then she clung to him. All the days of his life, he had received little but hard words and sharp actions from her, but now she burst into a terrible complaint, not in a screaming voice such as she had used before, but in a shuddering whisper, still holding close to him, clutching at his hands, or reaching up to stroke his head with her fingers, hard as bone.

'Child, child,' said White Crow. 'Big Hard Face is dying of grief. Besides what he has told you is not true. He is your father. He prayed to the Sky People for you. They heard him. They called him a great distance. They placed you before him. He took you and came back to his people. You are their gift to us. He has no child. I have no boy and no girl. If you go, we are like burned grass. We are like grass that has been burned by the roots. The wind blows us away from the earth. The moment you leave us, we begin to wait for our death. When you leave us, you kill us. Thunder Moon, have pity on me. Have pity on that old man!'

She fell upon her knees, clasping his hands.

'It is because I have said bitter words to you, like the old, wicked fool that I am,' moaned White Crow. 'But I have been evil in speech because I was jealous to make you the greatest warrior in the nation. I wanted to see you fly above the heads of other men, like an eagle. I always have loved you, and now. . . .'

Thunder Moon leaned and raised the withered body in his mighty arms.

'Do you think that I shall go?' he said. 'No, now I swear to you that. . . .'

'Thunder Moon!' said the clear, sudden voice of the girl. 'Ask your heart if you should swear. You have a real mother.'

The words were stopped on his lips, for into his heart was thrust a strange, new hunger which had been growing up there ever since the story of his foster father had been told to him earlier in the evening. He could tell himself that he was a Cheyenne and that he detested the whites and all of their ways. He even could tell himself that he loved his foster father and even that he was fond of the squaw, White Crow. But, at the same time, it was necessary for him to admit that he turned with all his soul toward the unknown man and the unknown woman who were his real parents. So the oath which he was about to take stopped in his throat.

White Crow, with a strangled cry of rage, rushed at the Omissis girl. Over her she stood, her fists clenched, and poured out denunciations in a screaming voice:

'You have stolen him!' wailed White Crow. 'Why do you want him? It is not for yourself. It is only to torment us. It is only to break the heart of Big Hard Face. There is no woman in the world so wicked as you are. You were a whip and wound to your father. You were like a winter wolf, eating your own kind. Now you come to eat us. But I shall·stop you. You will do no more harm to us or to others.'

As she spoke, she clutched the great war club which leaned against the post at the foot of the couch of the chief. Before Thunder Moon could stop her, she swayed the weapon over her head. The girl, like one recognizing doom, made no motion to avoid the stroke, but waited with calm, upward eyes. It was Big Hard Face himself who swept like a shadow from his place, and took White Crow, weapon and all, in his arms. Still she struggled. But she had begun to sob. Weeping overcame her and she lay in the darkness, moaning and beating her hands against her breasts, while Big Hard Face sat beside her, speaking like a mother to a child.

Thunder Moon stepped from the lodge as from a place of pestilence. The young men had vanished. All the camp was still. But in the neighboring teepees, he knew that many an ear was listening to the groans of the old squaw, and that the same ears had listened also to the altercations which preceded.

A soft step behind him, and he turned and looked down into the face of Red Wind. She bowed her head upon the tethering post that stood before the tent and leaned heavily against it.

'Are you not happy?' asked Thunder Moon, standing above her and towering in wrath. 'You have left everyone in the lodge of my father sick at heart. It is your work. When have you had a better day? Since the sun set on this day, you have stepped between me and Standing Antelope. You have broken the heart of my father. You have crushed White Crow, and you have torn me from my people. You have made me a man without a nation. I have no people. I have no heart. I am no more than a dead leaf blowing over the prairie. I am more friendless than an old buffalo bull, cast out by the herd. Tell me, Red Wind, is not this a perfect day for you?'

She did not raise her head, and her voice was a little muffled as she answered: 'Will you go then quickly? Will you go at once back to your own people?'

He was startled by this implied admission of all evil in her answer.

'After a little while,' said Thunder Moon, 'everything is understood even about the buzzard and the crow. They keep their lives because other things on the prairies die. So I know about you. You cannot be happy until you have driven me away from my people. But still you don't tell me why you hate me.'

'Listen to me,' said the girl, straightening and turning to face him. 'Already you have many enemies among the Suhtai. You are not a chief. You never will be a chief. Yet all the young chiefs are afraid of you and therefore they hate you. Snake-That-Talks has tried to murder you. He is a great young chief. Others are like him. They have pretended to love you, but they hate you. You have taken the son of Three Bears away and brought him back a warrior with a name. Do you think that Three Bears loves you because of that? No, he would bury his bullet in your heart if he dared. So it is with the others. You are white! You are white! You are white! Go back to the white men. You are not wanted here.'

Wounded vanity did not master Thunder Moon then. So many blows had fallen upon him recently that he was untouched except by the greatest things.

'There is only one thing that would keep me here, I think,' he answered her at last. 'That is to learn why you hate me, Red Wind.'

'Ask a woman why she hates and ask the wind why it blows,' said the girl savagely. 'All that I know is that I hate you. I do not want to be near you. Stand far from me, Thunder Moon.'

He hesitated over her, his breath coming in jerks.

'Do you wish to stab me when I touch you?' he asked.

'Once I have proved it to you,' she said.

'Yes, yes,' he nodded. He stretched out his hand and took in it the heavy, silken braid of her hair. It gave him strange pleasure and strange pain to see her wince from his touch.

'I have thought a little bit about women,' he said, 'but they have been good women that I thought I would take into my teepee one day. However, I cannot tell. It may be that this is the best. I have loved fighting and the war trail. But what is that danger compared to the danger of you, Red Wind? Ha! I know why your father gave you that name. It is because you are like a mist of blood blowing. You are like a cloud of fire sweeping through the sky. You are peril worse than poisoned air. Perhaps it would be a great pleasure to be hated by you. See, Red Wind, how much you are pleased to torture us. My life was a big life. When men looked at the Suhtai, they saw Thunder Moon first. The rest lived in his shadow. Now I am nothing. But perhaps I am pleased to torture you in turn. I touch you and your soul is sick. I think that I shall stay here and sleep among the Suhtai tonight and all the nights to come. Every night I shall not dare to close my eyes more than a wolf for fear of your knife and the knives of your lovers. By night and day I shall watch you to see that you take your poison into the life of another man. I have spoken. So let it be between us.'

Listening to him, she seemed eager once or twice to speak but, before he ended, horror seemed to master her. She began to shrink backward toward the entrance to the lodge. As he ended, she stepped past his view and disappeared into the interior of the teepee.

Still from the inside came the weary, endless sobbing of White Crow. It was impossible for Thunder Moon to enter that lodge upon this night. He went from the village and sat on the top of a hummock under the open heavens where he could have clear view of the stars which are the faces of the Sky People. He felt that this day had divorced him from everything that was old and tried and proved of worth in his life, and so he was pressed up closer to those invisible patrons who had sheltered him. The night grew old, and the high wail of a coyote on the horizon told of the coming of day. All the stars on the field of night began to wither and turn pale and small, but still he did not move from his place.

# 29

# Farewell

Men had failed Thunder Moon, and now the wide book of the sky, where always before he had been able to read some sign, offered him a blank. He rose from his watching with the feeling that he had come to the end of an old trail. In the cold, early dawn he came shivering back into the village. Even the dogs had not gained the courage that comes with the morning but only snarled at one another half heartedly, their tails tucked between their legs. The warriors were astir. Nearly a hundred braves had been assembled and were preparing to leave the village.

Thunder Moon's heart swelled with anxiety and anger as he noted the warpaint on their faces and all the familiar preparations which were only for a war path excursion of the first importance. In all the recent years not one such expedition had left the camp except that which had ridden to disaster against Falling Stone and his victorious Pawnees. With his single hand he had demonstrated that the medicine of Spotted Bull, who had excluded him from that trail, had been false medicine. But now another and a most important work was at hand and of it he had not been even apprised.

He gathered himself in his robe and stalked slowly through the mustering ranks of the warriors. With the utmost diligence they avoided his eye, busying themselves with their accoutrements and speaking eagerly to one another.

He could feel the glances of those who were in his rear turn after him, and he could hear their soft whispers. He felt the vibration of stifled laughter. They were mocking him behind his back. How long would it be then before they mocked him to his face?

He remembered what the girl had said. They did not love him, these Suhtai, no matter how many victories he had given to them. He could understand that that was the case. He was not one of them. Never had he felt the differences so keenly as now.

He passed Snake-That-Talks. Time had been when this doughty warrior would not so much as try to catch a prairie dog without first appealing for the advice of Thunder Moon. Now the brave regarded him with a sullen face and gave him no greeting whatever.

He passed Standing Antelope. The boy flushed with shame, but turned his head hastily away so that he might not see the older warrior.

At that the heart of Thunder Moon leaped in him. He drew his robe closer about him, and so came to the lodge of Spotted Bull from which the last of the selected warriors were issuing. The medicine man turned upon Thunder Moon with a broad leer of malice and triumph and the latter understood.

Once again Spotted Bull had made medicine which proclaimed that no fortune would accompany any expedition in which Thunder Moon rode. Once again he had been believed. Once more the insult was cast upon the shoulders of the warrior.

He endured it as well as he could. He walked on slowly, dying with an agony of injured pride and sorrow and despair. Yet he could see the reason for it all. In his own mind the history of past events which he had heard or witnessed remained as importantly as the tall forms of hills, ever present. But to the Suhtai and to all other Indians, the past was a pleasant or a terrible legend, the future was a misty dream, and only the present was of importance. What did it matter that Spotted Bull had been proved a lying impostor one day if, on the next, he seemed to dispel a thunder storm? So on the present occasion, he was believed implicitly when he prophesied that no good fortune could come to the warriors if they allowed Thunder Moon to ride out in their midst.

He went gloomily on through the village until he came to the lodge of his foster father. Big Hard Face sat in the teepee with Red Wind nearby, working or pretending to work at the beading of a pair of moccasins. White Crow was not present, and the warrior was glad of her absence.

He said briefly: 'It is time for me to go to see the face of my mother. Will you tell me how the trail runs?'

Red Wind did not look up, but her fingers froze at their work. However, the chief without alteration of countenance, leaned forward and began to trace his sketch for the journey on the ground.

For a quarter of a century he had not ridden over that ground, but now he was able to draw the plan accurately, presenting many details. He talked in terms of days' marches, and he drew in the main features that would be encountered, or else he sketched the chief landmarks by which the direction would be taken.

Another Suhtai would have carried all of these instructions written down in his mind. But Thunder Moon had no such gifts of visual memory. On a thin strip of antelope hide he reproduced the sketch as it was made to grow on the ground and then, rolling up the strip, he knew that he had his book of directions ready at hand in case of falling off the trail.

After that, he got his favorite dream shield, his war spear, his best rifle, and two revolvers. The weight of this equipment seemed out of proportion to the amount of food that he carried with him. But he must live by his weapons when he was on the road. Shooting is never so trained for straightness as when the day's pot depends upon it. So Thunder Moon was equipped for a great journey, and now he tried the edge of his hunting knife, and he adjusted his medicine bag, which was a little skin of a chipmunk containing, sewed up on the inside, a few small pebbles. He had not belief in medicine bags. His wearing of this one was simply a concession, pure and simple, to the necessities of bowing to the social will of the tribe. A man without a medicine bag was as inconceivable as a man without a head.

This bag he donned last of all of his equipment and when it was secured about his back, hanging by a thin rope of braided horsehair, he said to his foster father: 'This is a long trail. But I had better start on it at once. The young men of the Suhtai do not love me. I hope in Tarawa that they will not be crushed while I am away.

'If they ever should come to me to be helped, tell them that Thunder Moon is thinking about them, and that some of their faces and some of their words he cannot forget. They are marked down in his heart. Perhaps one day he will be written down in theirs. Now I start on a long trail where only one other Cheyenne has ridden before me. I know that I may leave my scalp on the way and my spirit go on before me.

'Therefore, my Father, let all things be clear between us. If you have given me a home and a name among the Suhtai, let it be said that I have given you love and obedience. If you have given me food and shelter for a long time, now I give to you everything that I have won by my hands, except Sailing Hawk and the weapons that I hold now, my saddle and the meat that I carry with me. But the beaded suits, and the rifles, and the painted robes, and the beads and the knives and the clubs and the captured medicine bags of our enemies, and everything else that I have, even to the eagle feathers which are used for the headdresses of chiefs and to ornament our shields, I give to you.'

Still Red Wind sat with her head bowed and her hands frozen at their work. The chief answered slowly: 'This is such a gift as a man makes when he is about to die. Do you go out with no hope, Thunder Moon?'

'No,' said the warrior, 'but I go with the knowledge that I must leave my old life behind me. That is well. I am not sorry. Some day I shall come back to you, and then I shall be all Indian or all white man. Now I am only a mongrel, neither wolf nor dog. The dogs snarl at me and the wolves have their teeth bared against me.'

'Farewell,' said the old man, raising his hand. From his pipe he blew a puff to the ground and another he wafted toward the sky. He handed the pipe to Thunder Moon, who imitated the example.

'Farewell,' said Thunder Moon.

He turned sharply on Red Wind. 'You have done much harm in this teepee,' he said. 'There still may be much harm left in you. There may be good also. You have driven me away. Stay here and help White Crow. She is old, and your hands are young and strong. As for me, I forgive you.'

She would not look up to him, nor answer a word, and he was rather surprised that her malice was so complete. He hurried from the lodge, a great lump in his throat. Just beyond the threshold he hesitated for a moment, for it seemed to him that he heard the stifled sobbing of a woman from the inside of the teepee. He told himself that it could be no more than the crying of a child in a neighboring lodge. He mounted the stallion and took his way through the camp.

# 30

# A Great Deal to Learn

He lingered for no other farewells but, heading straight across the open prairies toward the east and south, he settled the tall stallion to a raking trot that shuffled the miles rapidly behind him. North and west, in just the opposite direction from that which he had taken, he could see the dwindling cloud of dust which told of the war party, advancing slowly toward the realm of the hardy Pawnees. Again his heart swelled with indignation. Twice, as though in answer to his returning thought, Sailing Hawk slackened to a walk, tossing his head, and twice with a renewed resolution the warrior sent the stallion on again.

He had squared his shoulders against the back trail for some time when a regular pulse of sound behind him made him glance over his shoulder. He saw a rider coming at full gallop. A dim, dark hope rose in his mind that some enemy of his within the village, feeling that the medicine of Thunder Moon must have become very weak, had started on his trail to avenge some old disgrace. As the rider came closer, he made out in amazement the slender form of young Standing Antelope.

The latter, approaching swiftly, raised his right hand in greeting. As he came closer, he asked by sign if he could open a parley with his big friend. So Thunder Moon waved him in and Standing Antelope came to a halt beside him.

'The brave listen to the voice of Spotted Bull,' said the boy simply. 'I have listened too, and for a moment I forgot that Thunder Moon had given me my name, let me count my first coup, and call myself a man. I have given up the war party. I came back to ask you to forgive me. I found that you were gone. I was afraid that I never should find you again.'

'How did you pick up my trail?' asked Thunder Moon curiously.

'What other horse steps as far as Sailing Hawk?' asked the boy. 'Besides, he is not a bird, he makes a mark when he steps.' He pointed to the big, black, round hoofs of the tall horse, and Thunder Moon smiled a little. It eased his heart to see the keen eyes of this lad and to know that in this case, at the least, a lost friend had returned to him.

He said: 'I was going on a trail that may fill twelve moons. I never may return.'

'If I live to be a very old man,' replied Standing Antelope, 'I never can die better than by the side of Thunder Moon. If we are away for one snow, or for two, it is better. I may come back a man.'

'Turn back when you will,' said Thunder Moon. 'The trail will be long and, if your heart becomes empty and many marches are between us and the Suhtai, go when you wish.' The boy smiled at this suggestion that he might weary of the work and, drawing back two lengths and a little to the windward of his leader to escape from the dust, he followed obediently to the trail which his master had laid out.

Travel on the prairies is like travel over the ocean, with an unbroken horizon and no steady drift of landmarks past the eyes. By midafternoon the sun was sharp and hot. They had put many an hour of long, weary travel behind them. For all their labor they had no real sense of distance covered. All before them was as it had been when they left the Cheyenne village.

Now, however, a thin cloud of dust before them began to grow in size and distinctiveness. Standing Antelope volunteered to scout ahead, and he came back in an hour to report that he had made out a long caravan stretched across the prairie – a long host of wagons and riders, one behind the other, with outlying groups of guards or hunters riding over the plains.

'*If I am a white man,*' said Thunder Moon to his heart, '*why should I not join these people and journey along with them?*' He added aloud: 'Let us ride in and talk with them, Standing Antelope.'

'Ah, my Father,' said the youth, 'do you smile when you say this? Do not the Suhtai say that it is safer to trust the Pawnees than the whites?'

However, Thunder Moon insisted, and the boy, sitting stiffly in his saddle, most uneasy, followed his leader, his hand constantly upon his rifle.

Three hunters, returning toward the caravan with their horses loaded with antelope meat, now swept in toward Thunder Moon and came up close to him. They were like Indians in every respect, from buckskin, beaded shirts, to ornamental moccasins. The sun had darkened their skin, but the long hair which fell over their shoulders was not confined by a headband, and it was blonde and weather-faded. With their fierce, keen eyes, they estimated the value of the horse and the accoutrements of Thunder Moon. Every appointment was worthy of a chief and a great one, and the oldest of the three said, in fairly good Cheyenne: 'Suhtais, why are you here? Have you come to spy on us?'

That blunt question made the color fly into the face of Thunder Moon, but he said quietly: 'There is much hunting to be done for such a tribe as yours. Let me travel with you and hunt. You shall pay me as you please for the meat that I bring in with my friend.'

They looked at one another, murmured a few words, and then the oldest answered: 'Come in with us. We'll take you to the chief of the caravan.'

They rode on in the lead, while Standing Antelope followed at the side of his master.

He said with deft, swift fingers in the sign language: 'These three men want our rifles, and probably they want our scalps, and most of all they want Sailing Hawk. Even when they spoke to you, they insulted you with their first words and asked if you were a spy. Do not trust them, my Father! Three shots and they are dead. We count three coups, and we carry their scalps and their horses and their rifles away with us.'

'Their backs are turned,' said Thunder Moon.

'They are taking you into a trap.'

'Turn back if you wish,' answered the fingers of the warrior. 'I am going in with them.'

This challenge silenced the boy, but he was terribly ill at ease as they drew closer to the caravan. Now they could look through the dusty mist which boiled up behind the first wagon and settled in white sheets, streaked with sweat, on the animals that plodded in the rear, and on the other wagons, and on the men who rode or walked near the procession. Returning from the distant plains where they had been trading with the Indians, this caravan was chiefly loaded with buffalo hides. For weeks they had been on the way. For more weeks they would continue traveling. Considering the vast distances covered, the time spent, a white man would have wondered what profit could be in such trade. No such thought came to Thunder Moon. These toiling wagons, these unkempt men, ragged as wild Indians without their grace, were to him symbols of the white race, of toil, of slavery. Presently they came beside the rear-most wagon. There, striding beside a team of mules, was a monster of a man who turned aside at the hail of the three returning hunters and listened to what they had to say. All the while he kept his bold, pale eyes fixed on the face of Thunder Moon and, at last, he stepped forward and extended his hand. Thunder Moon took it, and instantly his fingers were almost crushed in a terrible grip. Almost crushed, but not quite and, regaining a slight purchase, by a desperate effort he held his own, then made his hand break into the powerful pressure which the white man exerted. He felt a tremor in the arm of the other; he saw amazement in the face of the stranger. Then his hand was suddenly set free.

'We can use you with our hunters,' said the white leader of the caravan, using a blundering Cheyenne dialect. 'But why are you here, my friend? Did you put a bullet into one of your own chiefs?'

He waited for no answer but strode away after his mule team. The three hunters, in the meantime, had found something in this interview which left them agape. Perhaps they were accustomed to seeing men crumple under the famous grip of the wagon boss. At any rate, they stared helplessly at Thunder Moon and at the faint smile which he had maintained throughout this brief and silent test of his manhood.

Then, suddenly, they began to smile at one another. He needed no knowledge of English to understand that he had been accepted in their society, and the first strain of apprehension was ended.

But what a society it was! During the day, he saw little enough of the teamsters and traders, for he was away across the prairies with the boy hunting. Only twice did they fail to find game. The instinct of Standing Antelope was marvelously sure and the gun of Thunder Moon was no less unerring when the game was in sight. But at night they sat at a camp fire and watched scenes so different from those in an Indian camp. The merry laughter and the childish free-heartedness of the

Cheyennes was replaced here by sullen, growling voices in a constant tone of complaint. After the supper was eaten, cards or dice appeared and games were played in silence, broken only by a snarl. Infinite danger was in those threatening voices. On the evening of the third day after they joined, they saw a revolver leap from a holster, saw the flash of the gun, and saw another man pitch on his face, quite dead.

Standing Antelope went aside with his leader shuddering. 'These people are like bad spirits,' he said. 'If they kill each other, soon they will kill us. See! There is no blood kin of the dead man to kill his murderer. No one cares. No one is excited.'

'They are gathering together,' said Thunder Moon. 'They have taken the weapons away from the killer. I think that something is going to happen.'

'Perhaps they are taking those weapons as a price for the dead man's life.'

'Perhaps. Let us watch, Standing Antelope. These are strange people. Who can tell what they will do? Who can understand them?'

'There is the chief coming.'

Loughran, the giant who had matched grips with Thunder Moon, came into the circle. Quickly he selected twelve men. He talked to them a moment. The twelve raised their hands with a solemn demeanor and made some answer. After that, half a dozen men came forward. They pointed to the slayer, but they were addressing the twelve. The whole period of the deliberations did not occupy more than half an hour. Then the hands of the prisoner were tied behind him and he was led out onto the plains a little distance, where a wagon tongue was fixed in the ground, with a rope passed through its upper end. The noose settled around the throat of the destroyer. In another moment he was suspended in mid-air, kicking violently.

'Let him down!' gasped Standing Antelope. 'They have punished him enough.'

'They are going to let him die,' murmured Thunder Moon, sweat standing on his brow.

'But then his spirit cannot get out of his mouth. It will die in his body and rot with his body if he is choked.'

'That is true,' said Thunder Moon. 'Look! He struggles no more. He is dead.'

'But were all the others blood relations of the dead man?'

'I shall ask.'

He stopped a passing waggoner and put the question. The latter said in answer: 'That is law, Cheyenne. No murderer has a friend in our country. We're all blood relations of the murdered man.'

'Law?' murmured Thunder Moon as they watched the body of the murderer cut down and buried with some care. 'What is law, Standing Antelope?'

'Death of the body and the spirit; death by hanging!' said the boy. 'I am very sick, Thunder Moon. Come away with me. I am afraid. These men are more brutal than beasts.'

'They are,' said Thunder Moon. 'But I think that there will be no more murders in this camp.'

Afterwards they went close to the spot where the dead man had been buried. They struck a light and found that a board had been put in the ground. Upon the board letters were carved with a knife.

'What does it mean?' asked the boy.

'It is medicine,' said Thunder Moon. 'This is a great medicine. What it means I cannot understand. But I shall never stop studying until I learn. Did you hear him? All are blood relations of a murdered man. That is law! Law, Standing Antelope, must be a great mystery. It is one of their gods.'

'The black robes do not talk about it,' observed the boy.

'We know nothing about these people,' said Thunder Moon. 'Let us watch closely. There is a great deal to learn.'

# 31

# Men of Many Minds

As the slow weeks of that journey went by, Thunder Moon began to learn the language of the whites by leaps and bounds. In the evening he picked up a new store of words. All the next day as he voyaged over the plains with Standing Antelope, he rehearsed what he had heard. When he returned in the evening, he attempted to use his stock. So his knowledge grew like a tropical plant, nursed by the heat of his great desire to know.

He was also learning far more than words, as a matter of course. Some ten days after he joined the train, he was wakened by a stealthy movement near him, and then he felt his rifle being withdrawn from beneath his pillow. He grappled with a shadowy form which crumpled under his grasp. When a lantern was brought, it was found to be a brute-faced teamster. Loughran, captain of the train, offered Thunder Moon his choice of two remedies. The first was that he, Loughran, would have the fellow stripped to the waist and flogged. The second choice would place the matter in the hands of Thunder Moon himself. Thunder Moon, seeing that the other was of a respectable bulk, accepted the second alternative. He was very angry. Moreover, he felt that these white men must be convinced, sooner or later, that he was a fighting man worthy of some respect. There was much amusement.

By lantern light the crowd made a circle. Into it stepped the combatants, and Thunder Moon glided close and smote the blow which was to begin and end the battle. He merely struck the air and received a hard fist in return, cunningly placed near the point of his chin, so that it felt as though a hammer had struck him in the back of the head.

For ten minutes Thunder Moon charged furiously at this elusive figure, while the spectators yelled with delight. But the brute-faced fellow seemed shot with wings. There was lead in either of his hands. He struck when and where it pleased him. One of Thunder Moon's eyes puffed and closed. His cheek was gashed. His jaw was lined with purple bruises. When he had his fury well cuffed out of him, he began to take time for thought. It was not through superior strength or courage that he was being beaten. It was by the medicine of the white man – it was by the mysterious use of mind. He took notice now that the first blow that the other threatened to strike never landed and the second one was what usually went home. So he re-made his own tactics. He let the feint of a left at the head go, then he stepped in, stopped, and smote for the body of his foe. Fair and square his fist landed. Bones crunched under the impact. A dreadful cry burst and broke in the air. The thief lay writhing on the ground.

Loughran tapped Thunder Moon on the shoulder.

'How did you learn that trick? He was a pug, Cheyenne!'

Thunder Moon did not understand, but what he *did* appreciate was that this battle gained him a new position in the camp. Thereafter all men treated him with a consummate respect. Certainly no more attempts were made to steal from him during the middle of the night. As for the pugilist, he was placed in a wagon, a very sick man, and transported groaning to the end of the journey.

There was no vital danger to the caravan except in one instance, and that was well-nigh both the first and the last. A sudden report came that Indians were sweeping toward them. Then out of a draw the charging warriors were seen to come, while the caravan hastily tried to double itself into a circle, the head drawing back toward the tail, and the tail rushing forward to join the head. Once formed into a circle of wagons, the caravan would take a lot of beating. If the Indians could insert the point of their wedge before the circle was joined, they could then open out the whole length of the caravans and slay as they pleased, as though a wildcat should sink its talons in the belly of a hedgehog before the little animal could roll into a ball. With wild shouting the wagons worked to make the circle, but they still lacked something of coming together when the first half dozen of the Indians on racing horses neared the gap.

There was no deference from within except from Thunder Moon. Chance had placed him at the vital spot and he did not think twice. Perhaps life seemed to him such a confused thing that he cared little whether he lived or died. At any rate, right through the closing gap in the wagons, with faithful young Standing Antelope scurrying behind him, he charged out at the enemy, shouting his war cry, a revolver in either hand.

They were Pawnees, chosen warriors. Yet to his amazement they did not wait for his charge. One among them shouted loud commands. The others split away to left and right and scurried back to join the charging mass of their companions. The next moment the circle joined – the wagon fort was complete. The Pawnees, not caring to try its strength, surged back to a safe distance and sat down like wolves to watch while a single chief came forward, calling in Cheyenne to Thunder Moon. The latter advanced, gun in hand, and he saw before him none other than that tried and famous enemy of the Suhtai, Falling Stone. The Pawnee leaped from his horse, threw down his weapons, and hurried forward on foot. His eye was gleaming not with hostility but with pleasure.

'Friend,' he said, 'my brother still lives and grows strong in his lodge, and every day he tells the Pawnees of the greatness of Thunder Moon. I have heard this story. If there is war between the Suhtai and the Pawnees, there is no war between Falling Stone and you. As for the white men, we should have split in between their wagons and eaten them as hawks eat mice. Now take a rich present from me. Take my rifle and my horse as a gift. Go off in peace with honor to the Suhtai. Leave me here to deal with these white men.'

'Falling Stone is a great chief,' answered Thunder Moon. 'But now I ride with these white men. They are my friends. If you fight with them, you fight with me. Be wise, Falling Stone. There are many guns in that circle of wagons. The men shoot straighter than Pawnees or Cheyennes. You will lose many of your braves and gain nothing.'

The Pawnee frowned and looked eagerly along the wagons, over which the dust cloud was beginning to blow away. Everywhere was the glint of rifles prepared for the battle. Then he nodded.

'I have lost a great prize for your sake,' he said. 'I would lose one still greater and yet be able to smile. But my gun and my horse are yours. Remember me for their sake.'

'Here,' said Thunder Moon, 'is a belt of beads for which I gave five strong horses. Take it, and remember me when you strap it on. If on another day we meet in battle, let us not see one another. There are other enemies for each of us.'

So they parted, Falling Stone walking off happily with the belt, and Thunder Moon taking his own prizes back to the wagon. He was received there like a hero. Whatever suspicion and dislike had surrounded him before now vanished and a crowd gathered to thank him for what he had done. There were more than thanks, however. When camp was made for that night, Loughran brought to him a good horse whose pack saddle was loaded down with all that an Indian could value. Guns, ammunition, knives, beadwork, sugar, coffee composed that load. Every wagon in the circle had made a contribution to the burden.

'Look!' said Thunder Moon to Standing Antelope. 'They are good people after all. They are not what they seemed at first.'

'You saved the price of a thousand horses,' replied the boy. 'They have given you the price of five. That is good business for them.'

The young Suhtai remained irreconcilable to the end. That end came not many days later when, as they camped at night, they saw far before them the glimmering lights of a town which was the end of the wagon trip. Half of the teamsters and hunters had scoured away to get to the waiting saloons in the town, and Thunder Moon and Standing Antelope went with them. Cautiously they moved through the crowds. They were not noticed. Other Indians stalked through the mob, unheeded. Everywhere was a confused turmoil of many tongues accented by occasional salvos of pistol shots.

After they had walked up and down through the noisy streets, Thunder Moon and the boy withdrew to the edge of the plains and the silence of the night.

'Now tell me about these people with white skins,' he said to Standing Antelope.

'No man can understand them,' replied the boy, 'because they have many minds in each head. One day they are great traders, the next they are foolish hunters. One day they are wise in council, the next day they chatter like foolish crows. One day they are rich with beads and robes, the next night they have given all that they possess for the sake of firewater which they put into their bellies, and it makes them sick. They are partly wise and they are partly not. Let us leave these people, Thunder Moon. We have each of us only one mind. Let us go back to the Suhtai where it is easier to know men.'

'Let us sleep,' said Thunder Moon sadly. 'In the morning we shall talk again.'

# 32

# The Reason Why

Morning came, the first gray touch of light. Thunder Moon, rising, saw that Standing Antelope was already up and had his horse saddled.

'Which way?' said the boy.

'Here is a horse packed heavily with rich things,' said the warrior. 'Take it and go back to the Suhtai. Here is enough to make you a wealthy man. You may have your own lodge and take wives. But I must go on. It is not what I want to do. But it is where I must go. The trail is not ended for me.'

'Go on, then,' said the youth. 'I cannot help following. I know that I never shall see my father's face again and Three Bears has only one son.'

However he could not be persuaded to depart, and straightway Thunder Moon turned more sharply to the south and east. Day by day they journeyed, now across open country, now they skirted the edges of the settlements of the whites, far advanced from the places where Big Hard Face had found them twenty years before. The landmarks which that hero had noted down were gone, almost without exception. Forests had been leveled. New ones had been planted and were half grown. Even Standing Antelope, to whom the story of the trail had been disclosed, was at a loss.

The time came when they had to leave the plains distinctly behind them and plunge straight in through the lands of the whites. They traveled entirely by night, sleeping fitfully through the day in some copse or heavy forest that they found. Now they crossed a region given over to the grazing of cattle chiefly, with great distances between the houses. Leaving that region behind them, they came to a district where the vegetation was richer. There was still a good deal of forest and there was a good deal of marshland, but all else was closely cultivated soil, the fields smaller and smaller, and hedged with walls of stone, or with rail fences. They would have had most difficult going here, on account of the marshes and of the many small streams, had it not been for the miracles of which Big Hard Face had told long before, and hardly been believed when he described them.

These were the roads which pushed straight ahead, regardless of obstacles, cutting through high or built up over low, and advancing through the marshes by causeways and over the rivers by means of great bridges.

Now and then too, they saw the sparkling lights of a great town in the distance. Once they lodged all day in a wood with the many noises of a large village murmuring or crashing about their ears so that they could not sleep.

It was easy to find food. With every house went a poultry yard, and in every poultry yard they could help themselves. If a noisy dog disturbed them at their work of foraging, the active knife of Standing Antelope quickly silenced the disturber. In this manner they went on, day by day, striking deeper and deeper into a strange country.

'If all the Sioux, all the Blackfoot, all the Comanches, all the Pawnees, and all the Cheyennes were gathered together and brought here, could they fill so many villages as we have seen?' asked Thunder Moon.

The boy shook his head.

'Still we are not at the end of the white man's country. How, Standing Antelope, can we beat these people in any great war?'

'By the help of Tarawa who gave us the plains,' said the boy confidently. 'Just as easily as we wring the throats of the fowls, so we could steal in and cut the throats of the sleepers in those lodges.'

Thunder Moon said nothing in reply, but he was beginning to have many doubts. All that Red Wind had said had come true and, though he had not as yet seen a 'medicine' canoe breathing fire and smoke, he was prepared even to see that.

Now they drew closer to their goal. All else on the landscape had been greatly changed, but the streams which Big Hard Face had crossed still flowed in the same places, and by that network of water Standing Antelope recovered the old trail.

By the march of half a night, they came at length about the middle hour of darkness to a great stretch of land where all the houses were gathered, as Big Hard Face had said, in the lee of a mighty mansion filled with lights. When they came still closer, they could examine the prodigious size of the house.

From its open door and windows – for the night was warm – music floated, a girl singing and the tinkling of some instrument that kept both the time and the key of her song with marvelous precision and beauty.

Thunder Moon listened, amazed.

'Why do you smile, Standing Antelope?' he whispered.

'Because it is not like anything that I have dreamed,' said the boy. 'I am afraid because it is unknown. Is it not a spirit that makes the music, my Father?'

'We will go to see.'

'Let me stay here. My heart is very weak.'

'Stay here then. I shall come again before long.'

He started away and Standing Antelope trembled alone in the darkness. Presently he heard a loud barking and a furious snarling from some dog apparently of the largest size. That clamor ended abruptly and the boy, with a faint smile, touched the handle of his knife. He also understood how to silence such a noisemaker.

After that he waited for a long, long time. The music ended, began again, ended and began again. A man was singing with the girl.

Finally Standing Antelope could stand it no longer but went forward to find his companion.

Across the open lawn he went, and through the hedges, and so he came closer to the house and the music and the singing throbbed in his very ears. He was vastly uneasy, for there was much light around the building. Through every window and doorway it poured out, and the young Suhtai made slow progress, creeping from shrub to shrub, hugging the shadows.

At last he saw a familiar silhouette – and it stood directly beneath a window. Very gladly Standing Antelope slipped up behind the tall warrior and, rising behind him, he looked at the scene whose fascination had turned Thunder Moon to stone.

He was peering into a large room. Seated at a music-making shape of wood was a girl with glimmering white shoulders and a tall youth stood beside her to turn big pages of paper. At the farther end of the room sat a gray-headed man and a white-haired woman.

All of this held little meaning to Standing Antelope, but he did understand in one breath why this long journey had been undertaken. The face of yonder gray-bearded man was the very face of Thunder Moon himself.

# About the Author

**Max Brand™** is the best-known pen name of Frederick Faust, creator of Dr. Kildare, Destry, and many other fictional characters popular with readers and viewers worldwide. Faust wrote for a variety of audiences in many genres. His enormous output, totaling approximately thirty million words or the equivalent of 530 ordinary books, covered nearly every field: crime, fantasy, historical romance, espionage, Westerns, science fiction, adventure, animal stories, love, war, and fashionable society, big business and big medicine. Eighty motion pictures have been based on his work along with many radio and television programs. For good measure he also published four volumes of poetry. Perhaps no other author has reached more people in more different ways.

Born in Seattle in 1892, orphaned early, Faust grew up in the rural San Joaquin Valley of California. At Berkeley he became a student rebel and one-man literary movement, contributing prodigiously to all campus publications. Denied a degree because of unconventional conduct, he embarked on a series of adventures culminating in New York City where, after a period of near starvation, he received simultaneous recognition as a serious poet and successful popular-prose writer. Later, he traveled widely, making his home in New York, then in Florence, and finally in Los Angeles.

Once the United States entered the Second World War, Faust abandoned his lucrative writing career and his work as a screenwriter to serve as a war correspondent with the infantry in Italy, despite his fifty-one years and a bad heart. He was killed during a night attack on a hilltop village held by the German army. New books based on magazine serials or unpublished manuscripts or restored versions continue to appear so that, alive or dead, he has averaged a new book every four months for seventy-five years. In the United States alone nine publishers now issue his work. Beyond this, some work by him is newly reprinted every week of every year in one or another format somewhere in the world. Yet, only recently have the full dimensions of this extraordinarily versatile and prolific writer come to be recognized and his stature as a protean literary figure in the 20th Century acknowledged. His popularity continues to grow throughout the world.